CALIENTE

DM BARRETT

This book is dedicated to Chef Rob Wilcox. He has prepared and served tens of thousands of great meals to Caliente members and guests.

Copyright © 2019 by D. M. Barrett
First Printing

A special note of thanks to my good friend, M.J., for the lovely images of her perfect feet in heels on the cover.

Published in 2019 by Horizon Press.

Cover design by: Mat Yan Cover Designs

Library of Congress Cataloguing
ISBN: 978-1-070-81407-0
Printed in the United States of America

Table of Contents

1. The Arrival

After leaving Tampa International Airport, it wasn't long before the resort shuttle approached the gates of Caliente Resort and Spa. The warm sunshine, gentle tropical breeze, and swaying palms were quite a contrast to the sub-freezing temperatures and snow-covered landscape of Minnesota.

It only took a week to convince Doc that his future was in Tampa not Minneapolis. It took another week to get their home listed for sale. By the third week, the two adult girls were fully vested in their parents' move.

A large ground mounted sign at the resort entrance to the walled community gave way to uniformed guards at the gate. A guard lifted the barrier and motioned for the shuttle to pass.

"Take us to the residence, please. We'll call a cart for the clubhouse in an hour or so," Dr. Michaels instructed.

"No problem," the driver responded.

The residence that had been bequeathed to Doc was a large one-story structure with a reddish beige tile roof and light beige stucco exterior.

As the couple opened the door, they were greeted by marble and hardwood floors, luxurious Persian rugs,

fine art on the walls, and expensive Victorian style
furniture. The dining room was furnished with a
twelve-seat dining table, hutch, and server topped by a
Tiffany tea set. The table was set with fine Astbury
black pattern china.

There was a large swimming pool, with fire bowls
and fountains, visible from the living room, den, and
master bedroom. A large ten-person spa was positioned
in the upper left portion of the screen enclosed patio.

The house consisted of a master bedroom, three
additional bedrooms, four full baths, and a three-car
garage. It was nestled amongst several dozen luxury
homes in the upscale neighborhood.

As Marilyn Michaels entered the master bedroom
she exclaimed, "There's even sheets on the beds!"

"There are linens in the closet, too," Doc remarked.

"Check the liquor cabinet and the pantry," his wife
instructed.

"There's enough liquor to open a store and there's
every type canned good imaginable in the pantry," Doc
observed.

"You call your mother and I'll get us registered and
our memberships paid at the resort office," Marilyn
instructed.

"I'll swap duties with you," her husband replied.

"Not for all the liquor in that cabinet," she retorted.

"It would be easier to write a chapter for a novel
than be on the phone with Waver for an hour," Doc
lamented.

Marilyn took her cell phone from her purse, dialed the resort office and asked, "This is Marilyn Michaels. Could you send a golf cart over to 69 Sandhill Crane Drive?".

"It will be here in a few minutes. Good luck with your mother," she said with a chuckle.

Doc picked up his cell phone and hit speed dial for his mother. She was unaware that her half- brother's property was located inside a clothing optional community and resort. Doc was not breaking that news to her – ever.

"Waver, this is your favorite son calling from the sunshine state," Doc announced.

"I bet that house is in rough shape. Your Uncle Donald was always a nasty housekeeper," Waver remarked.

"He must have had a maid or two. This thing is huge, fully furnished, and in great shape," Dr. Michaels reported.

"I suppose he put some of that Donald Duck Orange Juice money to work," Waver Michaels remarked.

While Doc continued the conversation with his mother, Marilyn was waiting to see the General Manager of the resort, Steve Riley. It might have been better for Doc if she had switched duties.

An attractive blonde lady opened the office door and said, "Ms. Michaels, Mr. Riley can see you now."

The pair walked through what appeared to be an office door directly onto a second story patio that overlooked the heart of the resort's 250,000-gallon waterfall pool, Tiki Bar, and outdoor stage.

As the two ladies approached, Mr. Riley looked up from his makeshift work area and greeted them. He was clad in a short sleeve floral pattern shirt and khaki pants. His laptop computer rested on a metal dining table with four chairs.

Steve Riley stood to welcome Marilyn Michaels, "We're glad that you and Doc are here with us. Donald Wales was a wonderful member at Caliente for the last fifteen years. We all miss him greatly."

"I never met Doc's Uncle Donald, but I've heard a few humorous stories about him," she replied.

"You can bet that they're all true. He was definitely a character," Mr. Riley replied.

"We need to register, pay our annual dues, and take care of all the business things," Marilyn reported.

"I think Anastasia has all the paperwork you need. If you will sign where she points and then give her a card, you will be good to go," Steve replied.

"While she is processing the paperwork, I want to ask a few questions," Ms. Michaels said.

"If I know the answer, I will tell you. If not, we'll ask Anastasia," Mr. Riley said with a chuckle.

"We saw in the brochures and on the website that the lifestyle is highly touted," Marilyn remarked.

"Caliente Resort and Spa is lifestyle-friendly but it does not sponsor or require lifestyle activities," the general manager explained.

"Doc and I are here for a change of pace. He needs something to challenge him. He had an active lifestyle before the accident. We need to get him back to there – the sooner the better," Ms. Michaels continued, "We even saw a lifestyle fitness center just a few miles from here near the University Square Mall!"

"We have our own fitness center that's open 24 hours a day, seven days a week," Mr. Riley replied.

"Do you have personal trainers?" she asked.

"We have two men and two women. You can interview them and choose the ones you prefer. The fitness center is included in your membership. The personal trainers are paid by the hour and charged to your Caliente account monthly," Steve explained.

"We are very, very excited about the lifestyle," Marilyn exclaimed.

"Does Doc really want to get into the swing of things so to speak?" Steve asked.

"I will see that he does," Marilyn said with a chuckle.

At this point it becomes obvious that Marilyn Michaels and Steve Riley are talking about two different kinds of lifestyle. Marilyn is interested in a healthy, diet and exercise program to aid Doc's recovery from the accident. Steve thinks she's talking about what was once called swinging.

"I will give your name and phone number to some of the local clubs and have them contact you," the general manager offered.

"Doc has always been an active member in several service clubs in the Minneapolis area. He needs more socialization and purpose in his life," she replied.

"There's always plenty of servicing needed here – especially on the weekends," Steve Riley said with a stifled laugh before continuing.

"By the way, be sure to visit our boutique downstairs. They have a great selection of exciting products," Steve suggested.

"I'm headed there now," she said as she stood to leave.

"Also, tonight is our Friday Meet-N-Greet. It's a great time to meet new friends both in the lifestyle and not in the lifestyle," Steve said.

* * *

After Doc finished his almost hour-long conversation with his mother, he decided to do some further exploration of the house that he inherited from his Uncle Donald. He was definitely in for a few surprises.

Doc rolled his wheelchair through the utility room to the door that exited into the three-car garage. In fact, there were three cars inside the garage!

There was a 700 series late model navy blue BMW coupe, a relative new maroon Lincoln Navigator, and a new, white Ford Escape. It looked like the inside of a car dealership show room.

Doc thought to himself that maybe his Uncle Donald bought the BMW to impress a few ladies, the Navigator to haul his girlfriends, and the Ford Escape for sharking for chicks relatively unnoticed.

While Doc further checked out the garage, Marilyn made her way to Lust, the resort's adult boutique. Needless to say that surprises awaited both of them.

Marilyn was welcomed into the boutique by a beautiful attractive blonde named Charlotte. She was very friendly and helpful.

"Come in and let us feed your man's lust," Charlotte invited.

"I'm in for that action," Marilyn replied.

"We have tons of sexy wear, hundreds of pieces of exotic jewelry, and dozens of different kinds of personal pleasure devices," the store manager announced.

"Oh my!" she gasped.

"Honey, we've got one called the cock-a-doodle-do. It's so good that if it could take out the trash, you'd give up men!" Charlotte boasted.

"What type of sexy swimwear do you have?" Ms. Michaels inquired in an attempt to change the subject.

"They are in those three wicker baskets marked small, medium and large. Just rummage through your size. It's like a garage sale over there," Charlotte suggested.

"Wow! They are really reasonably priced," Marilyn remarked.

"This is a clothing optional resort. Most folks exercise the option," she replied with a slight laugh.

"Where are the tops?" Marilyn asked.

"We don't cover up perfection," the store manager said with a large smile.

"I like this one. It's the right size and it looks like a leather thong," Marilyn said as she held up the small swimsuit bottom.

"It's actually vinyl and it's 100% waterproof. It's full of energy, if you get what I mean," Charlotte said.

"I'll take it. Do you have anything else on special?" Marilyn asked.

"Our newest and most popular line is called animal tails. We've got red fox, silver fox, raccoon, and skunk. The skunk inspired model has been the fastest seller. We call it the 'Little Stinker,'" Charlotte instructed.

Marilyn took the animal tail in hand and began to feel of it. It was faux fur but was very realistic. It had a small elastic band at the very end that looped around a clear, double knobbed piece of plastic.

"How do you wear it?" Marilyn asked.

Charlotte reached beneath the counter and placed a bottle of personal lubricant called Liquid Silk on the sales counter.

Upon seeing the bottle, Marilyn gasped, "Oh hell!"

* * *

Meanwhile back at the mansion, Doc had his first two visitors. It was two female neighbors who were taking their early afternoon walk through the neighborhood. Seeing that Doc had left the garage doors open, they realized that the Michaels had arrived.

The two well-endowed women went to the back of the house and knocked on the sliding patio door to get Doc's attention. When he wheeled toward the glass door, the two ladies crushed their bare breasts against it.

Doc opened the door and the two thong-clad women stepped inside. It was as if the road runner had just met two female road runners at once.

"I thought you were the Welcome Wagon," Doc said with a laugh.

"We're your naughty neighbors," the buxom blonde said.

"I don't know your names, but I'll know you when I see them . . . er, I mean you," Doc stammered.

"I'm Kimberly," the blonde replied.

"I'm Janice," the brunette said.

"It's a pleasure to meet your girls . . . er, I mean you girls," Dr. Michaels said.

"We sure miss Donald. He was a lot of fun," Janice remarked.

"Are you a lot of fun?" Kimberly asked.

"That's up for debate these days," Dr. Michaels replied.

"You come to the Meet-N-Greet tonight. We'll buy you a drink and we can get to know each other better," Janice invited.

"Bring your wife. We'll make her feel welcome, too," Kimberly promised.

Doc nodded as the ladies went out the glass sliding door and gave him a sexy wave. Those ladies are a hand-full he thought.

He heard Marilyn come in the front door and saw the she was carrying a small shopping bag that said Lust. The logo on the sack said: 'Lust Can Be Tamed But Rarely Conquered.'

"Is your lust tamed or conquered?" Doc said slightly sarcastically.

"I bought something to unleash your lust," she replied with a smile.

"Let's see what you got," Doc said.

"I was hoping you would say that," Marilyn responded.

She opened the small plastic bag, removed the faux leather thong, and held it up for her husband to see. It was very shiny in the well-lit living room and drew considerable attention from her husband.

"Is that leather?" Dr. Michaels asked.

"It's made of vinyl and it's waterproof," Marilyn beamed.

"Where's the top?" Doc inquired.

"This is a clothing optional resort, dear," she retorted.

"You're pretty close to exercising the option with that thing," Doc said.

"Do you like it or not?" the wife asked insistently.

"I'll need to see it modeled," Doc said wryly.

"Tomorrow, tomorrow, you'll see it tomorrow. We'll be at Meet-N-Greet today," she said paraphrasing a song from the Broadway show, Annie.

"Tomorrow is . . . another day," Doc said quoting Scarlett O'Hara from Gone With The Wind.

2. Meet-N-Greet

Doc was always well dressed but conservative in his attire. For the upcoming round of introductions to new friends and neighbors, he opted for a black polo style dress shirt a pair of dress pants with a very tiny hound's tooth pattern.

His wheelchair was black with subdued red trim. The frame was almost a candy apple red. It was built for looks and speed, The chair's model was a Quickie 2. It was functional with a futuristic look.

The one thing about the wheelchair that was destined be a conversation starter at Caliente was the company's logo on the back of the chair. It read: Everyone Loves A Quickie!

When Marilyn stepped out of the master bedroom into the living room, Doc got an eyeful — and more.

She was clad in a fire engine red dress, barely-there marching red high heels, and a pearl necklace, bracelet, and ring.

The red heels were mostly open and consisted of a few straps that held her nearly bare feet in position. Her French tip pedicure caused one to take a brief respite before following her shapely legs to the hem of the dress.

The dress stopped about mid-thigh and made it appear that her long legs made their way to heaven. On her left side it appeared to be a red version of the proverbial little black dress.

When Marilyn turned, the right side of the dress had six horizontal cut outs about two inches in height. The cut outs started at the bust and ended a few inches above the hem.

The first cut out gave a window to the side of her firm, slightly uplifted breast. Two other cut outs, one at the top of the hip and one lower on the hip completed a truly provocative look.

It was patently obvious from the right side view that only the red-hot dress was between her and the public.

"What do you think?" she asked with a mischievous smile.

"It has me itching and longing with desire," Doc said with a slightly elevated tone in his voice.

"That the effect I was hoping for," she responded.

"I have a prediction," Doc teased.

"I'm waiting for your vision of the future," Marilyn replied.

"When we get home from Meet-N-Greet that dress will hit the floor in less than 30 seconds," he predicted.

Marilyn opened the front door and nodded toward the outdoors. Doc didn't waste any time rolling his wheelchair through the front door.

While on his self-directed tour of the house he inherited from Uncle Donald, he located another vehicle. It was a mint condition electric golf cart that was built to look like a miniature two toned black and white 1957 Chevrolet.

"We've got at least 45 minutes. Let's tour the campus," Doc suggested.

"Like you always say, 'Let's see what you've got,'" she replied.

The Michaels' neighborhood consisted of several dozen luxury homes in the $750,000 to $1,000,000 range. The street entering the several blocks of dwellings was lined on both sides with luxury villas or town homes.

Each building, containing four villas, was a matching color to the other two dozen or so townhomes lining the street. The villas had garages and were in pristine condition.

One block down contained several blocks of luxury one- and two-bedroom condos. It was hard to get an exact count, but Doc's best estimate was that there were over 100 condo units in colors similar to those of the villas.

Almost across the main street as one approached the condominium complex was the entrance to several dozen small modular homes called casitas. Most had been modified or customized to include screened porches, large wrap around decks, and even additional rooms.

15

The color scheme of the casitas varied from those of the villas and condos. Nevertheless, they were color coordinated and mostly appealed to those who resided there only a portion of the year.

Caliente Resort and Spa owned rental property within each type of housing. The rentals were available for weekly or monthly stays for members and patrons desiring more space than was afforded in the resort hotel.

Doc piloted the golf cart onto the main street and turned left toward the Caliente Hotel and Clubhouse. Just passed the residential area was several tennis courts and a pickleball court.

Doc parked his 1957 Chevrolet style golf cart near the clubhouse entrance and gained access through a remote control on the exterior gate. It was truly like walking into paradise.

The lower portion of the resort complex contained a 250,000-gallon waterfall pool, a smaller pool adjacent to the Tiki Bar, and two large water volleyball pools. Palm trees provided both shade and ambiance to the tropical setting.

There were hundreds of lounge chairs that still contained a few sunbathers even though it was late afternoon. The Tiki Bar was still open to provide refreshments to members and guests.

The couple moved passed a large covered patio area with a huge spa and entered the building. In the center of the downstairs area was the adult boutique called Lust.

It was a glass enclosure on three sides. Their merchandise was easily seen by anyone passing the boutique. Given the late hour, it was closed.

To the immediate left of the boutique was the resort's day spa which offered a plethora of services, including but not limited to, different types of massages, body scrubs, facials, manicures and pedicures, and all types of skin care products.

On the immediate right of Lust was the resort's fitness center that Steve Riley had recommended to Marilyn. The fitness center was outfitted with every type of exercise machine imaginable. Marilyn noticed several patrons inside.

"We'll take the elevator directly to the piano bar. That's where the Meet-N-Greet is being held," she instructed.

"How long does it last?" Doc inquired.

"Steve told me from about 5:30 pm to 8:00 pm," Marilyn responded.

When the elevator door opened, there were about a dozen people seated in the tall bar chairs at the tables. The group ranged in age from mid-thirties to late sixties.

The men were dressed similar to Doc. The women were clad in what Doc would eventually and affectionately refer to as 'slut wear.'

"It looks like it's gonna be a slow night," Doc opined.

"Give it a chance. It's early yet," Marilyn replied.

"It's kind of sleepy, too," he suggested.

"It's a piano bar. It's supposed to be mellow so people can talk and visit with each other," she retorted.

While Doc went to the large, well-stocked bar area at the back of the room, Steve Riley appeared and made his way toward Marilyn. He was wearing dress slacks and a short sleeve dress shirt.

"Are you enjoying yourselves?" Mr. Riley asked.

"It's a little slow. We were hoping for a little more action," Marilyn replied.

"Just give it a little time. I really doubt that you'll be leaving disappointed tonight," Steve promised.

Doc returned to the table. He was followed by a young, cute, college-age waitress bearing two drinks. Marilyn could tell that one was a glass of white wine.

"What are you having?" she asked.

Before Doc could respond, the waitress said, "A Shirley Temple."

"I guess he's living life on the ragged edge," Marilyn said rolling her eyes.

Ignoring her comment Doc asked, "What did your man have to say?"

"That was Steve Riley, the general manager. He said the entertainment and activities will get better as the night goes on," she reported.

"A little excitement wouldn't hurt one bit," Doc said.

At a nearby table two attractive forty-something ladies overheard Doc's remark. They both turned in the direction to get a better look at the couple.

"Sounds like that guy in the wheelchair is good to go," the redhead said.

"I'd definitely take a test drive," the blonde replied.

"When his woman leaves the table, I'm going to see what I can work up," the redhead said with confidence.

Marilyn decided to walk across the room and speak with Anastasia, the assistant general manager, and Charlotte, the boutique manager. It gave the girls and opportunity to speak with Doc.

"Damn, Marilyn! That's one hot little red outfit," Charlotte opined.

"That'll cause some excitement tonight," Anastasia remarked.

"Doc said it would hit the floor within 30 seconds of going through our front door," Marilyn said with a chuckle.

"I just hope you make it home tonight unmolested," Charlotte replied.

While Marilyn and the ladies continued their somewhat risqué banter, the two ladies at the table near Doc were busy plotting an introduction. They decided that the redhead was going to be the bait to get Doc's attention.

"Hon are you ready to go?" the attractive redhead inquired.

"I'm close but I should probably stay a little longer," he replied.

"Well, let me and my friend know when you're ready. We'll take you with us," she said.

"What's your entertainment tonight?" Doc queried.

"Are you up for a rodeo?" she asked.

Not realizing the veiled offer, Doc responded, "I love a rodeo, but we have other plans tonight."

"We're ready any time you see us," the attractive redhead stated.

Marilyn started walking toward Doc. The redhead returned to her table and seated herself next to the blonde.

"What did she want?" Marilyn inquired.

"Well, I think she wanted to determine when this table would be available," he said.

"What else did she say?" Marilyn asked.

"She invited us to a rodeo, but I told her we had other plans tonight. She said that they were ready anytime that we saw them," Doc reported.

"I didn't realize that rodeos were popular in Tampa," she said.

"This is a fairly cosmopolitan place. They may have been from Texas," Doc opined.

In a few minutes a very attractive buxom brunette took a seat at Marilyn and Doc's table. She was clad in a translucent black mini dress and sky-high heels.

"I hear that your man is a doctor. What's his best skill?" the brunette asked.

"He's a dentist. He mostly does pulling and filling," Marilyn replied.

"Honey, I got two that need pullin' and one that needs fillin'," she replied.

"I'm recovering from an automobile accident. I wouldn't be able to help you, but I can probably find someone who could," Doc replied.

"I think I'll just wait for you," the brunette said as she exited the table area.

"Marilyn, you don't need to be drumming up dental work in Florida. I'm here to rest and relax. I don't need to be providing services to our neighbors," Doc said with slight irritation.

"I've never met that lady. She seemed to have a lot of confidence in your work," Marilyn responded.

"Steve may be the culprit. He wants us to be happy and well liked apparently," he opined.

A well-dressed middle-aged cowboy approached the table. He was clad in cowboy boots, jeans, western shirt, and a large cowboy hat.

"How are you doing tonight, little lady?" the Texan asked.

"I am soooo excited to be here," Marilyn replied.

"I was wondering if you'd be able to help Ol' Tex tonight?" he asked.

"What do you need?" Marilyn asked with a puzzled look.

"I'm looking for a high-spirited little filly," Tex said.

"Any particular kind?" Doc inquired.

"A hot brunette that really enjoys a good ride," the Texan explained.

"We're new here, but I'll keep my eyes and ears open," Marilyn said with a smile.

"Indeed," Tex replied.

Tex made his way to the nearby table where the attractive redhead and blonde were sitting. Doc watched them share some pleasant conversation and then they left the table and exited the piano bar.

"Meet-N-Greet may have been a bust for us but that Texan made friends with those two rodeo girls," Doc observed.

"They all liked western things like horses and rodeos. Maybe they're from Texas," Marilyn remarked.

Charlotte approached the table introduced herself to Doc. She was a tall, attractive, pleasant blonde that was as Doc would say, well put together.

"I'm Charlotte. I sold your wife a black thong bikini today," she said.

"I saw it. It was quite nice," he replied.

"Nice? I was hoping it made you get out of that wheelchair and yell, 'I'm healed!'" Charlotte said with a laugh.

"It could happen. I haven't seen it on her yet. She said the modeling is tomorrow," Doc replied.

"So, when does that hot dress hit the floor tonight?" she asked bluntly.

"It's about seven or eight minutes to the house and about 30 seconds thereafter," he responded.

22

"I'm calling the wholesaler. Lust has got to get some of those. You'll be lucky to get her home before the rodeo begins," Charlotte remarked.

Charlotte said her farewell and made her way to another part of the room. Anastasia waved but did not approach their table.

Looking at his watch, Doc said, "It's about ten minutes till the dress drops!"

Marilyn signed for the bar charges. They headed for the elevator and downstairs to the golf cart.

As they drove home Marilyn asked, "Did you have fun tonight, dear?"

"I think it was fine. I think Tex probably had a lot of more fun at the rodeo," Doc said.

"Meet-N-Greet is a weekly event," Marilyn reminded.

Marilyn opened the front door and stepped through. Doc was close behind her.

Marilyn dropped the red dress from off her shoulders and stood silently. It didn't take more than two seconds for Doc to turn off the light.

"Now this is my kind of Meet-N-Greet," Doc said.

3. Morning and Evening (Part I)

It was approaching noon when the doorbell rang. Marilyn peeked through the curtains and saw a handsome, blonde man standing at the door.

"Who is it?" Doc inquired.

"It's not the postman," she reported.

"How do you know?" Doc asked.

"He's nude and has four gold rings on his schmeckle," Marilyn said.

"Open the door and see what he wants," Doc said.

"I'm naked!" she exclaimed.

"Just keep him away from the dining table. He may try to steal Uncle Donald's gold napkin rings," Doc said with a laugh.

Marilyn opened the door. Neither she nor her visitor spoke immediately.

"My name is Mako Jenkins and I want to invite you out," the gentleman said.

"What does he want?" Doc asked as he rolled toward the entrance foyer.

"He wants a date!" Marilyn exclaimed.

"Then he definitely likes your outfit," Doc said tongue-in-cheek.

"I'm the president of the homeowners' association. I want to invite you and Dr. Michaels to Tiki Bar Karaoke today and a costume party tonight in the nightclub," Mako explained.

"My husband sings a little and I love parties," Marilyn exclaimed.

"Great! I'll meet you at the back gate at 1:00 pm today," Mako said as he nodded and turned.

Doc made it through the large dwelling and to the front door just as Mako was leaving. When he reached the curb, he turned and waved before walking down the street.

"What happened?" Doc asked.

"A date to Tiki Bar Karaoke and the nightclub costume party tonight," Marilyn said as she closed the door.

"I guess he liked your forty-year-old ass," Doc opined.

"Your name didn't come up, dear," she retorted as she walked toward the master bedroom.

* * *

Doc and Marilyn met Mako at the resort's back gate at precisely 1:00 pm. They exchanged pleasantries and Mako invited them inside. Doc wore a pair of light gray canvas shorts and a lavender colored polo shirt. He had on white sneakers and socks.

Marilyn was partially exercising 'the option' as she was sporting the black faux leather thong swimsuit with black spike heels. Her sexy look was completed with a gold and black onyx necklace, onyx bracelet, and matching ring.

"Are you a nudist?" Mako asks.

"She just plays one on TV," Doc replied slightly sarcastically.

"She's definitely in character today, brother!" Mako exclaimed.

The resort was filled with guests and members. Doc estimated that in lounge chairs and the four lower pools there were close to 500 people.

"We usually have a live band on Saturday and Tiki Bar Karaoke on Sundays. There was some sort of scheduling problem so this week the days got switched.

The trio made their way through the sunbathers and past the pools on their way to the Tiki Bar. The music started when they were about 50 feet away.

Marilyn and Doc recognized the song being sung as Sharp Dressed Man by ZZ Top. The inebriated singer had changed the words and crooned: "Every girl's crazy 'bout a well-hung man."

Slightly embarrassed, Mako excused the impromptu lyrics by saying, "It's just karaoke."

"Sounds like drunky-oke," Doc responded.

"That, too," Mako replied.

As they made their way to the Tiki Bar's double doors, Steve Riley was there enjoying the frivolity. He looked at Marilyn and nodded his head approvingly.

"Doc come sing us a song" Steve said loudly.

The crowd chanted, "Doc! Doc! Doc! Doc!"

"I've been consummated, and you are the prime suspect, Mako Jenkins," Doc accused.

"Be a good sport, dear. Sing us a song," Marilyn chided.

Doc rolled to the KJ booth and introduced himself to KJ Nick Colorado. He was playing some music videos between the few people brave enough to hold a microphone that afternoon.

"What do they want to hear?" Doc inquired.

"Whatever you sing," Nick replied.

"I'm not very good," Doc reported.

"It's karaoke," Nick said.

"I've heard," Doc said with a sarcastic tone.

Doc selected a song and the KJ handed him the microphone. It was heavy, wireless, and appeared to be of very good quality.

"Any instructions," Doc inquired.

"That's my best mic. It's reserved for real singers. Don't dare do a mic drop it could result in an ass whooping," Nick instructed.

"Bring a sack lunch. It'd likely be an all-day job," Doc retorted.

Doc rolled to the Tiki Bar stage and the music started. He had chosen a Stevie Ray Vaughan classic entitled: The House Is Rockin'. He crooned:

Well, the house is rockin', don't bother knockin'
Yeah, the house is rockin', don't bother knockin'
Yeah, the house is rockin, don't bother, come on it

Needless to say it only took the first verse to get the Tiki Bar rockin'. Women were dancing. The few who were wearing swimsuits started hurling them at Doc.

There were a few ladies rubbing against him. One even straddled him in the wheelchair.

During one of the instrumental breaks, Nick announced, "That man has tremendous concentration!"

He continued his lovely little rock and roll ditty:

Walkin' down the street, you can hear the sound
Of some bad honky-tonkers, really layin' it down
They've seen it all for years, got nothin' to lose
So get out on the floor,
Shimmy 'til you shake somethin' loose

As Doc's performance neared its conclusion, a very buxom, naked young woman with an athletic build made a flying leap into Doc's lap. Unfortunately, the momentum tipped the wheelchair over backward with the two of them intertwined.

Although the performance became legendary at Caliente, two facts were never omitted when the story was told: (1) Doc never missed a note and finished the song on his back, and, (2) Doc held tightly to DJ Nick Colorado's expensive microphone.

Mako Jenkins looked at Marilyn and opined, "That man's a hit!"

"No doubt," Marilyn said with a chuckle.

Mako came to the stage to greet Doc and compliment him. It took a few minutes for him to make his way through the crowd.

"That was great, Doc. It was really good," Mako exclaimed.

"It's karaoke," Doc said with a smile.

The two men made their way to the bar to order libations. The actual bar was a concentric circle in the middle of the thatched roofed circular structure.

"What for you gentlemen?" the bartender asked.

"My wife will have a glass of Merlot," Doc replied.

"What can I get for you, Doc?" he asked.

"What do you recommend?" Doc inquired.

"We've got beer that's colder than your ex-wife's heart," the bartender boasted.

"Damn, that would be a beer-sickle!" Doc exclaimed.

"I want a Pabst Blue Ribbon beer-sickle," Mako said.

The barkeeper looked at Doc and said, "He's from Georgia."

"I'm from Minnesota and I'll have the same," Doc responded.

A tall, white haired gentleman approached the bar and introduced himself, "I'm Bruno Eberhardt. I must speak to you about your singing."

"What's on your mind?" Doc queried.

"I think you should sing some longer country ballads," Bruno opined.

"Why do you feel that way?" Doc asked.

"So it will make the women emotional and I will have time to proposition them," Bruno explained.

"I will keep that in mind," Doc promised.

The two men shook hands and Bruno moved to a different part of the Tiki Bar. Mako looked at Doc and shrugged.

"Is that fellow from Germany?" Doc asked.

"He's from Iowa. His name is really Kleinz," Mako replied.

"Where does the name Eberhardt come from?" Doc queried.

"It's a play on phonetics. Eberhardt is like ever hard," Mako explained.

"I didn't look down," Doc said.

"I did," Marilyn interjected.

"Was it the eighth wonder of the world?" Doc asked slightly sarcastically.

"It probably has its own zip code," Marilyn opined.

* * *

Marilyn excused herself and made her way toward the ladies' room beside the eight outdoor showers. She noticed a man and woman using colored ropes to bind women in a decorative manner.

When she returned from her brief respite, she stopped to watch the gentleman engage is his unusual art form. It was quite an attraction to Marilyn.

"Would you like to be bound?" the young woman asked.

"It would be my first time for something like that, but I have to admit that it's quite intriguing," she replied.

"I'll see that you are next in line," the young woman responded.

When Marilyn stepped to the spot where the man was performing his skill, he took a few moments to decide what type of decorative bondage scheme he would employ. He opted for some rainbow-colored cotton rope and full standing immobility.

"My name is Cameron and I see you've met April," he said.

"I'm Marilyn. That guy singing 'The House Is Rockin' is my husband, David" she explained.

"I've decided that I'm going to do a nautical theme with you," Cameron explained.

"That sounds exciting," Marilyn responded.

"You have no idea," April said with a large smile.

Cameron took the rainbow-colored cotton ropes and began wrapping them around Marilyn's legs, waist, and arms. He tied a knot in a length of rope that went from her back to her front, between her legs, and then affixed it firmly to her bound hands.

"Can free yourself?" he asked.

Marilyn struggled but couldn't make any headway in gaining her freedom. She was tied in an upright, standing position and completely immobilized.

"Why do you refer to this as a nautical theme?" Marilyn asked.

Cameron grasped the portion of the rope that went from her front to her back and between her legs. He began moving the rope up and down. The knot hit just the right spot.

"I say it's nautical because the fish is pulling on the line making the bobber, meaning the knot, go up and down," Cameron explained.

"Your bobber is definitely getting attention," Marilyn acknowledged.

"Honey, do you like the theme?" April asked.

"A few more minutes of fishing will be all that I can stand," Marilyn said with a slight shortness of breath.

Marilyn's brief respite and her interaction with Cameron and April took longer than expected.

When she returned to the Tiki Bar Doc said, "We thought you'd run off with another man."

"I got . . . I mean I was . . . er, tied up by a couple I met," she said with a stammer.

"Was it a pleasant experience meeting them?" Mako asked.

"He was very knowledgeable about fishing and nautical knots," she replied.

"I've never known you to have any interest in fishing," Doc said with a puzzled look.

"I guess it's all in the technique," she replied.

* * *

The sun started going down and the temperature began to cool. Marilyn and Doc thanked Mako for the day's outing and returned to their home to get ready for the costume party. The doors at nightclub opened at 8:00 pm but the word was that the party really started humming at 9:00 pm.

Mako spent another hour at the clubhouse before leaving. He made his usual rounds delivering insight and humor. He just did what caused him to earn the nickname Mako.

He was always on the move checking out the women. Many people referred to it as sharking. Thus, Mako Jenkins earned his nickname.

This week's themed party was a costume party. It encouraged members and guests to come dressed as their favorite character.

By the time they arrived home, Marilyn decided to wear a costume called Greek Goddess. It consisted of a white dress with a plunging neckline, a gold crisscross with small cutouts on the bodice, and gold trim on the short sleeves.

She added a gold coiled serpent armband and a gold serpent necklace. Her shoes were strappy gold flats with bands that wound past mid-calf.

When she modeled the outfit for Doc it created some slight controversy. The dress was about six inches above the knee and the outfit was quite provocative as a whole.

"What do you think?" Marilyn asked.

"You've dressed for the holidays!" Doc exclaimed.

"What holidays? What are you talking about?" She asked.

"It must be the holidays. That short hemline is showing everyone that it's close to Christmas," Doc replied.

"That may be, but if you keep talking, you'll be getting a lump of coal tonight," she replied.

Doc grunted but didn't utter a word. He knew that discretion truly was the better part of valor.

"What is your costume tonight?" Marilyn asked changing the subject.

"I'm going with a Christmas theme, too," Doc responded.

"You're gonna pick that scab again?" Marilyn asked sternly.

"Really, I'm wearing my Jesus clothes: robe, tunic, sandals, wig, and crown of thorns," Doc explained.

"No you're not," she said.

"I'm not? Who am I going to be?" Doc asked.

"You're going to lose that wig and crown of thorns," Marilyn instructed.

"What will that do for me?" Doc inquired.

"It'll turn you into Caligula." she replied.

"When in Rome," Doc said with a sigh.

* * *

Gilbert temporarily parked the six-passenger resort golf cart at front of the Caliente Clubhouse. Doc and Marilyn were greeted by two sculpted marble lions standing guard at the entrance.

It wasn't long before they heard from the resort's mascot, a parrot named Pedro. When Marilyn turned sideways to exit the cart, it was quite a leggy exhibition. Pedro made a loud, shrill whistle that sounded like the traditional wolf call. Several patrons turned to get a view of Marilyn.

"That bird's got good taste," Gilbert remarked.

"Indeed," Doc replied.

Gilbert retrieved Doc's wheelchair from the back of the golf cart. Doc made a quick transfer and started rolling toward the glass double front entrance doors.

"I do," Gilbert said with Doc giving him double thumbs up.

"What's he talking about?" Marilyn asked.

"He saw the back of the wheelchair that says, 'Everyone Loves A Quickie,'" Doc replied.

They were met at the resort entrance by a gentleman who introduced himself as Dave McDonald. He was a younger, middle aged man with a pleasant smile and a happy demeanor.

"Mako is having dinner with his wife in the diner," Dave said pointing to their left.

When Doc and Marilyn turned to see the restaurant, they quickly decided that Dave was using the word diner as a dysphemism. It was obviously more than a diner.

Las Palmas had about 20 four-chair tables covered with white tablecloths, rolled black napkins, and sparkling silverware. The upper level of the restaurant had another dozen similarly set tables and a few semi-hidden booths.

The restaurant was about 75% occupied with several well-dressed servers taking orders and delivering food and beverage.

Mako and his lovely wife, Beverly, waived from an upper level table. Doc returned the wave and Marilyn blew a kiss.

"This is an SBBC weekend," Dave remarked.

"What does that mean?" Marilyn asked.

"That's the acronym for Sexy Bare Bottoms Club. They're a lifestyle social club that provides clothing optional travel opportunities and social gatherings for its members," Dave explained.

"What type of travel opportunities?" Doc inquired.

"Nudist cruises, topless destinations, and a monthly lifestyle party or event," Dave responded.

"Do they live up to their name?" Doc asked with a hearty chuckle.

"There's a few with some hail damage but not many," he opined.

Before anyone could respond, Dave temporarily excused himself. It appeared that a tall, thin, attractive redhead had caught his attention.

"Hail damage? What did he mean that a few had some hail damage?" Marilyn queried.

"Cellulite, those dimples on some women's asses," Doc replied.

"Well, I certainly don't have hail damage," Marilyn said with a slightly raised voice.

CALIENTE   DM BARRETT

"If a slight breeze catches that short dress, the crowd will know it, too, since you are without benefit of panties," Doc remarked.

"I'll make sure they enjoy the Christmas scenery," a somewhat irritated Marilyn responded.

Dave returned and apologized for his brief hiatus. He happened to recognize, Diana, a lady he had dated years before.

"Let me take you on a short tour while Chadwick, our food and beverage manager, has the staff ready your Club Fiesta table," Dave offered.

"I would love a tour," Marilyn said.

The couple walked past both the nightclub entrance and the piano bar area. Several ladies smiled and waved, and a few men smiled and nodded.

"Are they your friends?" Doc inquired.

"They are your fans from earlier today," Dave suggested.

"It was just karaoke," Doc replied.

"Indeed," Marilyn remarked.

The trio exited the double glass doors at the rear of the piano bar. They stepped onto a large balcony that wrapped around the entire rear of the clubhouse.

To their left was the glass enclosed Calypso Cantina, the resort's sports bar. On their right was Club Fiesta with its multi-colored lights and shiny mirrored ball flashing through the large glass windows.

As they stepped forward, the balcony gave a view of the four lighted pools, the Tiki Bar, and the large sunbathing area. It was impressive as the many palm trees swayed in the very light tropical breeze.

"Have you seen the upper pool and large hot tub?" Dave queried.

We thought that four pools were enough. We weren't aware of a fifth pool and second hot tub," Marilyn remarked.

"The lower pools are mostly for swimming, wading, volleyball, and an occasional quick dip for cooling down during sunbathing stints. The upper pool is a conversation pool," Dave explained.

"Is that where deep geo-political discussions are held?" Doc asked with a smile.

"It's where men give women ear-gasms," Dave said.

"What are ear-gasms?" Marilyn inquired.

"During the day, women, in various stages of undress, give men eye-gasms. After dark, men engage in meaningful, poignant conversation with women and give them ear-gasms," Dave theorized.

"Maybe we can get in the conversation pool later and Doc can improve his technique, she remarked.

"No doubt," Doc responded with a noticeable sigh.

4. Morning and Evening (Part II)

Doc, Marilyn, and Dave McDonald stood on the balcony outside the nightclub and watched dozens of couples enjoy the warm water of the hot tub and the conversation pool. It was obvious that the upper deck was the place to be after sundown.

Chadwick stepped to the outside door of the nightclub and said, "Dr. Michaels, your table is ready.

"We're on our way," Doc replied.

The trio made their way to the flashing colored lights, shiny mirrored ball, and past the patrons to their table. It was a round table with three chairs. Chadwick had wisely removed a fourth chair so Doc would have a place to park his wheelchair.

Doc's place was on the left side of the table. Marilyn seated herself on the right side. Dave McDonald chose the rear chair remarking that he always kept his back toward the wall.

Shortly after being seated, Doc was approached by a middle-aged blonde wearing a black leather teddy decorated with two pair of handcuffs at the waist, black spike heel leather boots, and carrying a black whip. She sat squarely in Doc's lap without saying a word.

"Can I help you?" Doc asked politely.

"I want to tie you up," she replied with a German accent.

"Why is that?" Doc inquired.

"You have been a naughty boy and you need some discipline," she said.

"I think you have me confused with that gentleman at the bar, Bruno Everhardt. He's been quite naughty," Doc urged.

"Then I will apply the appropriate measures," she insisted.

Doc was somewhat relieved as she walked toward the bar to confront Bruno. They spoke briefly and then left together.

"What did she want, Doc?" Dave asked.

"She said she wanted to tie me up because I had been naughty," Doc explained.

"Was she serious?" Marilyn asked.

"When a woman comes at me with handcuffs and whips, I take it seriously," Doc said without hesitation.

"What did you say, Doc?" Dave asked.

"I told her Bruno Everhardt had been very naughty. I guess she found him a more tempting target," Doc said.

"I know a lot of women that would find him tempting," Marilyn remarked.

"No doubt," Doc said with slightly raised eyebrows.

After about an hour, and after the music and noise level increased, Chadwick came to the table and explained, "We now have a padded booth about 20 feet from the dance floor. It seats four and you are welcome to move."

"Doc take the booth. It'll be more comfortable. I've promised to meet Diana at the hot tub at 9:30 pm," Dave said.

Doc nodded and Chadwick moved the couple to the padded booth closer to the front door of Club Fiesta. The booth was very comfortable and afforded them the opportunity to converse with the dance music more in the background.

A very muscular couple entered the front door of the nightclub. The lady noticed Doc's wheelchair behind the booth and walked toward the booth.

"My name is Dee Sanders. This is my husband Jack Sanders. I am a personal trainer," she explained.

"Both of you be seated. I'd like to speak with you about what I need," Doc replied.

"Would you mind if I dance a few dances with your beautiful wife while you two discuss business?" Jack inquired.

"That's fine with me. But you should ask her next," Doc suggested.

"Before words were exchanged, Marilyn left her seat at the booth and offered Jack her hand. He graciously helped her off the booth's raised platform and escorted her through the club to the large circular dance floor.

Dee seated herself beside Doc. She slid tightly beside him.

"Steve Riley, the general manager, told me that you were interested in the lifestyle. Is that correct?" Dee asked.

"I have some interest but it's more at my wife's insistence," Doc replied.

"That's often the case," Dee said.

Thinking the discussion was only for a diet and exercise routine, Doc asked, "So how should we begin?"

"You don't waste any time," Dee said.

"A procrastinator is rarely successful," Doc explained.

Dee lifted her shirt to display her very trim, muscular chest. She had small breasts with large nipples.

"Feel them," she instructed.

"I can't feel them. Your husband is on the dance floor with my wife," Doc protested.

"He doesn't mind, and your wife insists, according to Steve," she replied.

Thinking she wanted him to notice her toned, athletic body as a sales point, Doc reached and fondled her right breast and nipple.

"Do they look good and feel good for a 42-year-old?" Dee asked.

"They are perfect for a 21-year-old," Doc said as he fondled the personal trainer's other breast.

Dee had closed her eyes to enjoy the experience. Moments before Doc had finished his assignment, a salt and pepper haired middle-aged gentleman appeared beside the booth and stood next to Dee.

"What's going on?" the gentleman asked.

Dee opened he eyes and displayed a look resembling fearful excitement. She recognized the man as her next-door neighbor. He was aware that she was a free-lance personal trainer but was unaware of her other activities at Caliente.

"I'm a doctor. I'm giving Dee a free breast exam," Doc quickly replied.

"That's my next-door neighbor, Mr. Rogers," she squeaked.

"And it's a beautiful day in the neighborhood," Mr. Rogers replied.

Doc encouraged Mr. Rogers to join them but he opted to see if he could find someone to ask to dance. Both Dee and Doc started to breathe easier.

Marilyn and Jack returned to the booth after dancing to four or five songs. Jack looked very pleased and Marilyn looked a bit disconcerted.

"Did things get handled?" Jack asked.

"Indeed," Dee said as she drew air.

"Did she meet your expectations?" Jack inquired further.

"And then some," Doc said with a slight chuckle.

Before anything else could be said, Dee reported, "Mr. Rogers was here and saw us."

"How did he react?" Jack asked.

"He said it was a beautiful day in the neighborhood. I took that as positive," Doc replied.

"No doubt," Jack said as he looked at Dee.

"We should let Doc and Marilyn enjoy some time together. We need to make our rounds for the evening," Dee suggested.

As soon as the couple left the table, Marilyn looked at Doc and said, "He groped me."

"A little or a lot?" Doc asked.

"Does that matter?" Marilyn asked with a tone of disbelief.

"It depends on whether you liked it or not, I suppose," Doc replied.

"He mostly checked for hail damage," she said.

"No wonder he was happy," Doc remarked.

"He checked to see if the grass had been mowed too," Marilyn said just above a whisper.

"Good that it was mowed recently," Doc said with a laugh.

"You're incorrigible," Marilyn replied sharply.

"I was trying for that effect," Doc replied.

"It's getting late. We need to say goodbye to Dave McDonald," she instructed.

* * *

As they arrived at the large hot tub and moved to the side when Dave and Diana were located, Dave asked, "So what have you two been up to?"

Before Marilyn could respond, Doc replied, "Marilyn met with the handy man about hail damage and lawn care."

"You're a horse's ass," she replied to Doc.

"You can throw a pretty good saddle," Doc responded with a smile.

"Marilyn, let me introduce you to James Ritz. He's a charter boat captain. He's standing by the steps over there," Dave suggested.

"He looks interesting," she replied after taking a long look at the captain.

"He was a well-respected mechanical engineer. After success with a couple of patents, he left engineering and decided he wanted to be a charter boat owner and captain," Dave explained further.

"I like fishing and nautical themes," Marilyn said.

"So I've heard," Dave replied.

"I may try a dip in the spa," Doc announced.

"Do you need me to get the lift?" Dave inquired.

"It only has three steps. Just hold the chair so it doesn't tip while I transfer," Doc replied.

"You don't have to lose your inhibitions, but I recommend that you lose those clothes or risk the chemicals giving them a fade job," Dave warned.

Doc moved his wheelchair at a slight angle to the hot tub stairs, stood up, and grasped the metal rail. He moved to his right and placed his right foot on the top step followed by his left.

He repeated that procedure twice until he was able to sit on the circular bench inside the hot tub. He seated himself and gave Dave the thumbs up.

"Wow! That's some technique that Doc has there," Dave exclaimed.

"He has better techniques than that," Marilyn said as she raised her eyebrows.

"Doc keep an eye on Diana. I'm going to introduce Marilyn to James and go get a beer," Dave asked.

"Not a problem," Doc said.

After Dave and Marilyn walked toward the upper deck steps, Diana moved closer to Doc. She hopped into his lap and positioned herself on his left leg.

"Have you ever had an international flight attendant in your lap?" she asked.

"Once during turbulence over the Bay of Biscayne but she was fully dressed," Doc replied with a smile.

"Well, I'm nekked," Diana stated.

"You mean you're naked – without clothes," Doc suggested.

"No, I'm without clothes and I've got naughtiness on my mind. I'm nekked," she responded.

"I think I see the difference," Doc said.

Suddenly, a beautiful blonde in her early forties hopped on Doc's lap and positioned herself on his right leg. Doc was starting to get a little nervous. Other than Marilyn, he was unaccustomed to having a naked woman in his lap. Tonight, he had two that were drop dead gorgeous.

"I'm Marlene. How are you doing tonight?" the blonde asked.

"It seems I have just doubled the pleasure and the fun," Doc said.

"That's my friend Marlene. She was a playmate in the 1998 November issue.

"I can see why," Doc stammered.

"Have you ever had a naked playmate in your lap?" Diana inquired.

"Not even a clothed one," Doc replied.

"Have you ever had a three-way kiss?" Marlene asked.

"I'm not sure what that is but I'm sure I haven't," Doc admitted.

Both girls leaned toward Doc. Marlene planted a kiss on the right half of his lips and Diana planted a kiss on the left half of his lips.

When the brief kiss was over, Marilyn was standing in front of the trio. She had her arms crossed. Her face had a penetrating look.

"I wanted to introduce you to James Ritz. But it appears that you're busy," she said with a rather icy stare.

"Doc, it appears you have your hands full," James Ritz said with a hearty laugh.

Nodding to his left, he said, "This is Diana. She's here with Dave."

Nodding to his right, he said, "This is Marlene."

Before anything else could be said, Marlene remarked loudly, "I'm here with you, baby!"

"Not for long, dear," Marilyn retorted.

"Who's that chick, Doc?" Marlene asked.

"That's my wife, Marilyn," Doc said rather sheepishly.

"Come on, Marlene, let me show you the conversation pool," James invited diplomatically.

Marlene stood up, hugged Doc and gave him a big kiss right on the lips. She hopped out of the hot tub and walked toward the upper pool with Captain Ritz.

Before anything else could be said, Dave appeared with a Pabst Blue Ribbon in his hand and stepped into the hot tub. He saw a little tension but no drama as he approached the three.

"Everything going OK, Doc?" Dave inquired.

"He's the center of attention tonight," Marilyn remarked.

"Diana, give Doc a break. Let's take a dip in the conversation pool and cool down," Dave recommended.

As they walked away, Doc felt the proverbial noose tighten around his neck. He was braced for the jolt at the end.

"I'm waiting on the best explanation you have," Marilyn stated harshly.

"Diana is redheaded international flight attendant. Marlene is her friend. She's a blonde Miss November 1998 Playboy Playmate. I've never met a man that wouldn't let two naked beauties like that park themselves in his lap for ten minutes," Doc explained.

"What about the kissing?" Marilyn asked with a significantly calmer tone.

"I didn't have the heart to damage her self-esteem," Doc explained.

Marilyn grunted and gave a slight nod to Doc.

"Am I in trouble?" Doc inquired gingerly.

"No, you're every man's hero and every woman's object of desire tonight. You have seen everyone on the upper deck gawking at your naked ass. I'm not going to play the villain in this soon to be legendary story," Marilyn responded.

"What are your plans?" Doc asked with a puzzled look.

"Get you home and make sure you don't have those two hot chicks on your mind for long," Marilyn said with a smile.

Marilyn retrieved Doc's wheelchair and locked the wheels. Doc worked his way to the hot tub stairs, grabbed the rail, and worked his way up the steps and to his chair.

Marilyn took his large Caliente beach towel and quickly dried him off. Doc seated himself in the wheelchair.

Doc rolled up the long ramp and to the gate. Marilyn walked beside him. They waved and nodded to several members and guests on the way to the remote gate.

While they waited for the gate to open, Marilyn asked, "What did you expect when you saw me standing there after having a three-way kiss with those two women?"

"I thought to myself: If I get my ass busted, this is one time it's worth it just to be able to tell the story the rest of my days," Doc replied.

"I'm sure your version will be better than actually being there," Marilyn responded.
"If it's true, it's ain't braggin'," Doc said followed by a hearty laugh.

5. Sunday Morning Coming Down

Doc and Marilyn were awakened by the obnoxious sound of a ringer for a 1950s era telephone. For nostalgia's sake, the ringtone was readily available on most smart phones including the Apple models.

"What's that?" Marilyn asked without opening her eyes.

"It's Waver calling my phone," Doc said with a sleepy tone.

"Let it ring," Marilyn suggested.

"She'll call every five minutes for the next hour," Doc predicted.

"What time is it?" Marilyn asked.

"Time for me to crawl my naked ass out of this bed and talk to Waver," Doc responded.

"Hello Waver!" Doc said in a cheerful tone.

"Did I wake you up?" Waver asked.

"Of course not, we've been up since 6:00 am feeding the chickens and slopping the hogs," Doc said sarcastically.

"Your Uncle Donald never overcame being a Tennessee redneck. Who else would have chickens and hogs in Tampa, Florida?" Waver asked with incredulity.

"We've decided to give them to a couple from Georgia we met yesterday," Doc continued.

"What do they do?" Waver asked.

"As little as they can," Doc replied.

"That explains why they need chickens and hogs," Waver remarked.

"What's got you buzzing so early?" Doc asked.

"Your brother brought his little prissy girlfriend over and took me to breakfast at Cracker Barrel," she reported.

"What's the occasion?" Dr. Michaels asked.

"They told me they were getting married," Waver exclaimed.

"That's wonderful news!" Doc said excitedly.

"Well they've been fornicating for three years in that townhome of his. There'll be nothing new but the license!" Waver exclaimed.

"Waver you are just mean spirited. Your redneck is showing,"

"My redneck is showing but at every Vikings football game Amber's ass is showing,"

"Mother, she is a professional cheerleader and Roger is the team physician," Doc responded.

"Every time she kicks up her heels on the television you can see the outline of the mouse's ear," Waver said sarcastically.

"Waver, you should be more considerate. Amber will be your daughter-in-law someday," Doc scolded.

"She needs to put on some clothes! Your father didn't see that much skin until our wedding night. She acts like she's in a hoochie-coochie show," Waver said in a raised voice.

"Waver, you need to calm down. This conversation is not helping your blood pressure. You'll have a stroke and die," Doc instructed.

"Well, if I do, make sure that strumpet wears some real clothes to my funeral," Waver said.

"I love you, Mom. I hear the dogs barking. Tell the preacher to pray for you." Doc said as he ended the call.

"What's got her so wound up this early on Sunday?" Marilyn asked.

"Roger and Amber took Waver to Cracker Barrel and announced their engagement," Doc reported.

"We should have looked to the north for a mushroom cloud," Marilyn remarked.

"She was livid. She went full Tennessee redneck," Doc said.

"Well, she lived in east Tennessee, and you and your brother got admitted to schools in Minnesota," Marilyn replied.

"Over the years, we've tried to fade our rednecks, but Waver wears hers like a red badge of courage," Doc said with exasperation.

"Roger has been more successful than you," she responded.

Doc's phone rang again. This time the ringtone played "Satisfaction" by the Rolling Stones.

Recognizing that as Roger's ringtone, Marilyn remarked, "Now you can hear the rest of the story."

"Congratulations, Roger. I'm very happy for you and Amber," Doc announced.

"Thanks, brother," Roger responded.

"I got the redneck version from Waver. I'm ready to get the rest of the story from you," Doc said.

"Waver acted very southern and quite hypocritical. She was so sweet that sugar wouldn't melt in her mouth," Roger reported.

"She'd been sucking on the hot sauce by the time she got to us," Doc replied.

"I really need to talk seriously to you about things," Doc's brother said.

"Say on," Doc replied.

"We've decided to avoid the big wedding and the Waver controversy that will inevitably happen. We're getting married in Maui and honeymooning there for a couple weeks before returning to Minneapolis," Roger said.

"I think that's great," Doc said excitedly.

"You may not think it so great since Waver will be down there with you for two weeks," Roger said.

The conversation stalled with almost a minute of dead silence. Doc replayed in his mind what had just been said to make sure he heard his brother correctly.

"She can't come here. This is a nudist place and it's edgy, too!" Doc exclaimed.

"I can't help it if you decided to live in Uncle Donald's house there in Sodom," Roger said.

"Actually, it's more like Gomorrah, but that's beside the point," Doc responded.

"The bottom line is that you have to watch Mom for a couple weeks. You're resourceful. You'll figure something out. I'll call back in a few days and give you all the details," his brother explained.

"This is going to be a train wreck," Doc exclaimed.

"Grab the throttle and drive on, Casey Jones," Roger said as he terminated the call.

"What's Roger's story?" Marilyn inquired.

"He's eloping with Amber to get married in Maui and taking a two-week honeymoon," Doc reported.

"That is so romantic. It's just wonderful!" Marilyn exclaimed.

"It is definitely romantic but far from wonderful," Doc replied.

"Why would you say that?" Marilyn asked.

"He's sending Waver here for the two weeks," Doc said.

"Oh fuck!" Marilyn exclaimed.

"Fuck me!" Doc responded.

"What's she gonna say when she finds out that this is a clothing optional resort?" Marilyn asked with shock.

"David, you and Marilyn might as well call Hell and make a reservation. Don't waste time. Talk to the Devil directly," Doc said in a voice mimicking Waver's.

"I need a mimosa, Marilyn exclaimed. Let's get ready and go to Café Ole for Sunday Brunch," she suggested.

Doc didn't respond to her comment. He just kept looking at the floor.

"Are you all right, David?" she asked.

"Now I understand the real meaning of Johnny Cash's song, 'Sunday Morning Coming Down'," Doc said somewhat philosophically.

"What is it?" Marilyn asked with a puzzled look.

Doc replied rather rhythmically:

"On a Sunday morning sidewalk
I'm wishin' Lord that I was stoned."

"Get ready, Johnny, help is nearby," Marilyn replied.

* * *

Doc opted for a fashion trend he's just noticed at Caliente. Men would wear a floral-patterned button up oversized shirt, shoes and socks, but no shorts. Doc was told it was called "shirt cocking."

"What are you wearing?" Marilyn yelled from the bedroom as she decided on an outfit.

"I'm shirt cocking," Doc yelled back.

"I don't know what that is but I'm supportive," Marilyn said.

In about half an hour, Marilyn emerged from the master bedroom wearing a copper toned beaded skirt, a pair of matching striped wedge style shoes, and matching jewelry. Her makeup and hair were perfect.

The beaded mini skirt had several strands of miniature beads that surrounded her from her waist to the top third of her thighs. The strands dropped down about 14 inches from her waist toward her knees.

"What do you think?" Marilyn asked.

"A large percentage of the guys at the clubhouse will be interested in what's behind the curtain rather than Monty Hall's cash," Doc replied.

"That's the effect I was hoping for, but Caliente is a cashless resort. Everything goes on your house account," Marilyn said as she walked to the door with the beaded strands swaying.

"What about the girls?" Doc asked referring to her breasts.

"Charlotte, the lady at the boutique, said that we don't cover up perfection at Caliente," Marilyn replied.

* * *

The pair decided to take the walking path for the short distance from the house to the restaurant. It was a warm 75 degrees and sunny in the early part of February in Tampa.

"How are you doing in that beaded skirt?" Doc asked.

"My sexy almost bare bottom is catching a breeze," she replied.

"I've got to look away. I'm starting to get a little motion sick," Doc responded.

In only a few minutes, the couple arrived at Café Ole. They were quickly seated at one of the white tablecloth-covered tables. Apparently, the restaurant was Café Ole for breakfast and Las Palmas for lunch and dinner.

The server arrived at the table and Doc said, "Two mimosas, please."

"David, you don't drink. Why did your order two drinks with champagne and orange juice?" Marilyn asked.

"The orange juice is in memory of Uncle Donald and the champagne is to celebrate Waver's visit," Doc replied sarcastically.

"You better plan on a screwdriver and go to vodka and orange juice the day she arrives," Marilyn retorted.

"No shit," Doc said.

* * *

After the couple had finished their brunch, they decided to take a lounge seat at an upper deck palapa. The umbrella shaped thatch roof provided ample shade for the pale skinned Doc while permitting Marilyn to sunbathe intermittently.

It wasn't long before Marilyn opted for a piña colada from the upper deck bar. Doc asked for a Shirley Temple.

While Marilyn waited for her order to be filled by the buff bartender, she was approached by two thirty-something ladies. Both had golden-tanned hard bodies. They were wearing nothing but smiles.

"We apologize for our curiosity, but we were wondering why your husband is in the wheelchair?" one of the beautiful Latin ladies inquired.

"He was in a very serious auto accident almost a year ago," Marilyn replied.

"How is he doing?" the second lady asked.

"He's in much better shape physically but he still suffers with bouts of depression," she explained.

"Does he enjoy motor boating?" the first Latin lady asked.

"He loves boating. It's one of his favorite things," Marilyn responded.

"Is he able to get up?" the second Latin lady asked.

"He does pretty well but he needs a little help occasionally," Marilyn reported.

Upon hearing her response the ladies looked at each other and excused themselves. They made their way across the upper deck and toward Doc.

The handsome, blonde, muscular bartender leaned over the bar and said to Marilyn, "He might be able to handle one Latin woman but he damn sure can't handle two!"

Marilyn watched as the first lady, who she eventually learned was named Maritza, straddled Doc, pushed his face between her bare breasts, and gave him a good long shimmy.

"Your wife said you'd love to go motor boating," Maritza said.

"I've been motor boating in both Minnesota and Tennessee, but I like the Caliente kind the best," Doc exclaimed quite red faced.

As Maritza uncoiled herself from around Doc, the second Latin Lady, named Crystal, took position and took him for his second motor boating of the day.

When Crystal had finished her task, Doc said, "This was quite a vigorous trip for a Sunday!"

"We'll let you rest and check back later," Maritza replied.

"Indeed," the slightly breathless Doc said.

Marilyn returned to the palapa with the two piña colada drinks. Doc was quite red faced partly from the excitement of the motor boating and partly that she'd watched.

Marilyn handed Doc a piña colada instead of the Shirley Temple that he'd requested. He gave her a strange look to alert her that she'd gotten him the wrong drink.

"Don't give me that look. You went from Dr. Michaels to Captain Morgan and took two trips to the islands," she remarked.

"But I . . . I mean . . . they said," Doc stammered before Marilyn interrupted him.

"Calm down and drink up, Captain. You can search for the booty later at 69 Sand Hill Crane Drive. There'll be a wench waiting for you. Aaaaaarrrgh!" she responded with her best pirate impersonation.

When he finished his piña colada, Doc determined that it might be a good time for a brief respite. He excused himself and rolled toward the restrooms.

As Doc exited the facilities, his buxom blonde neighbor, Kimberly, came up behind him and wrapped her bare breasts against his ears, leaned his head back, and asked, "Guess who?"

"It's one of my naughty neighbors playing headrest with me," Doc said with a chuckle.

"Did you peek?" Kimberly asked.

"No, but I recognized the size, shape, and luxury size of your headrests," Doc responded.

"I'm happy you enjoyed the experience," Kimberly chided.

"But of course!" Doc exclaimed.

After a short conversation Doc excused himself and headed back to the palapa. The upper deck was starting to get crowded and the pool and hot tub were filling for Skinny Dip Sunday.

"Is everything okay?" Marilyn inquired.

"Why do you ask?" Doc queried.

"Your ears are red, and you face is flushed," she explained.

"It may be the sun. The angle is different in Florida from Michigan," Doc suggested.

"It could be that earmuff session you just had with that big breasted blonde, too," Marilyn said tongue-in-cheek.

"Actually it was a luxury headrest session," Doc said.

"Let's go, Captain. You've been on enough excursions today. Besides, you need to get your wench to surrender the booty," Marilyn explained.

"No problem," Doc said as he rolled away into the warm Florida sunshine.

6. Ladies' Night

Doc heard the doorbell and rolled toward the front door to answer it. When he peeked through the window curtains beside the front door, he saw Mako standing there in all his glory.

He did not hesitate to motion him inside. Mako took a few steps and made his way into the large living room.

Out of nowhere a small, male Pomeranian dog stands on his back legs and wraps his front legs and paws around Mako's right leg. In a matter of seconds the little dogs began his affair with the nude man's lower left leg.

"That dog is humping my leg," Mako said with slight irritation in his voice.

"He won't take long," Doc said with a reassuring smile.

Marilyn heard conversation and made her way to the living room. When she arrived, she was horrified that the little dog was, in her words, making love to Mako's leg.

Before she could say anything, the little dog released his embrace and stood there smiling at Mako. However

Mako did not share the joy of moment with the Pomeranian.

"Oh, I am so very sorry, Mako," Marilyn said.

"I hate to trouble you, but do you have a tissue?" Mako asked gingerly.

As Marilyn scurried to the master bathroom for some wet wipes, the two men and the dog stared at each other. Only the dog seemed to embrace the moment.

"I didn't notice your dog the last time I was here. How long have you had him?" Mako inquired.

"He's Mike Anderson's dog. I'm watching him for a few hours while he makes arrangements to take the dog with him to St. Martin, French West Indies," Doc explained.

"What's the dog's name?" Mako asked.

"He's called Bonheur (pronounced boo-**nair'**). It's French for happiness. But I call him boner," Doc replied.

"He had one and didn't mind puttin' it to use this morning," Mako remarked.

"Indeed," Doc responded.

Marilyn returned with a box of wet wipes and began to wipe the fruit of Bonheur's loins from Mako Jenkins' lower left leg. Doc watched with interest as Marilyn gave an occasional glance at his four golden ring-encased schmeckle.

"Doc, you sent me an email about a special guest you expected next week. I came over to talk about it," Mako explained.

"My 75-year-old mother, Waver, will be staying here for a week while my younger brother is on his honeymoon," Doc replied.

"Hell we'll have a big block party with suds and tunes," Mako exclaimed.

"Here's the problem: She doesn't realize that her half-brother lived in a luxury, clothing-optional resort. We don't want her to know that we live in a naked neighborhood either," Doc explained.

"Wow! That is a problem," Mako said with a chuckle.

"If you put it in the weekly newsletter, the story may deter the neighbors from dropping by unannounced or without clothes," Marilyn said.

"If she did find out, what would be the fall out?" Mako asked.

"She'd say that we might as well rent this house and live in hell because that's where we're headed," Doc said.

"Damn! That's cruel," Mako said.

"Indeed," Marilyn replied.

"I'll get the warning in the newsletter. It goes out tomorrow," Mako said.

"Are you going to write about Bonheur?" Doc asked with a wry smile.

"I don't want to violate the dog's privacy," Mako said in a monotone voice.

"Well he enjoyed violating you," Marilyn retorted.

Gently changing the subject Mako said, "Are you guys coming to Ladies Night tonight? It's your first. Drinks are free for ladies from 8:00 pm to 10:00 pm."

"We'll be there. I'm wearing a fishnet teddy," Marilyn remarked.

"Mako can bring his decorative rod," Doc remarked.

"On that note, I will see you at the nightclub about 8:00 pm tonight," Mako responded.

The trio said their goodbyes and Mako started out the front door. Bonheur wagged his tail and barked approvingly.

"He's saying it was good for him," Doc said teasing Mako.

"Tell him to enjoy St. Martin," Mako said walking down the sidewalk and onto the street.

* * *

"Do you think Mako was offended by Bonheur's actions?" Marilyn asked.

"I doubt it was his first bad sexual experience," Doc responded.

"David, that's rude," Marilyn scolded.

"No, what Bonheur did was rude. What I said was truthful," Doc responded.

"In any event, we need to talk about Waver's visit. She'll be here in two days," Marilyn implored.

"She has reservations on the last flight from MSP to TPA. That should put her arriving at 11:59 pm Eastern," Doc replied.

"So we can bring her in under cover of darkness and she'll see no naked people at that time of night," Marilyn responded.

"We'll turn left and come directly to the house. It's very unlikely that they'll be anyone nude in this area that late," Doc reminded.

"What about the rest of the time?" Marilyn inquired.

"That's a work in progress," Doc said with a chuckle.

"Let's have some lunch at the Sports Bar and do a little shopping at Lust," Marilyn suggested.

"Let's satiate some lust and then hit the Sports Bar," Doc offered.

"Take that up with Bonheur or roll up to the boutique with me," Marilyn replied.

"I'll go with you. Bonheur needs to pace himself," Doc said.

* * *

Upon arriving at the Caliente Clubhouse, Doc suggested that Marilyn get a head start at Lust while he checked out Caliente's Spa Sereno. The pair parted ways briefly to complete their assigned tasks.

"Are you ready for another week of lust?" Charlotte asked.

"I'm ready for a lifetime of lust," Marilyn replied with a laugh.

"You need to plan a healthy sexy-wear budget," Charlotte recommended.

"My husband refers to it as slutwear," Marilyn reported.

"I'd say slutwear is more provocative than sexy-wear," Charlotte replied.

"I want pure slutwear. I want outfits that you can't wear anywhere but here," Marilyn said.

"You are definitely at the right place," Charlotte said while Marilyn started looking through the boutique.

Doc asked for the spa manager. He said he wanted to make an appointment for Marilyn for later that afternoon. She replied that she could explain the spa's various services and make the appointment herself.

"What kind of spa services are you interested in for your wife?" she asked.

"I want her to get a couple hours of pampering," Doc replied.

"I recommend a soak, a full body scrub, and a massage," the receptionist replied.

"How long will that take?" Doc asked.

"It about 30 minutes, 50 minutes, and 50 minutes," she responded.

"That's just a little over two hours. It's perfect," Doc replied.

"When do you want her services to start?" she asked.

"She's got about 30 minutes at Lust and about an hour for lunch. Let's get her started at 2:00 pm," Doc replied.

"Who's going to take care of her?" Doc asked.

"My recommendation is Paul. He's excellent. He's twenty-eight years old, strong, muscular, handsome, and a good conversationalist," the receptionist reported.

"Ring it up. I want to give him a large gratuity. Hopefully, he'll give her extra special service," Doc explained.

When he was handed the bill to sign, Doc added a $100 gratuity for Paul. Upon seeing the tip, the receptionist smiled and nodded her head.

Doc rolled out of the spa and a short distance to the boutique. Marilyn had a pile of resort wear for his approval.

She had picked out three outfits that she really liked. Charlotte euphemistically referred to them as "sexy wear". Doc was fully convinced that they were slutwear of the highest order.

The first outfit was a sheer black mini dress in the front, a black strap around the back of the neck to hold it in place, four black straps across the upper back, and six black straps across her bottom.

There was an elongated gold tone triangle holding the upper black back straps in place and a similar triangle starting at the top of the derriere holding the bottom six straps in place.

"We want it," Doc said abruptly.

"I haven't told you the price," Marilyn replied.

"Don't interrupt his lust. He's on a roll," Charlotte pleaded.

The next item was an almost neon yellow cat suit with a deep V neckline. In fact, it appeared that it was going to be difficult to keep her breasts covered most of the time.

The yellow cat suit could be open at the crotch or closed by an almost invisible piece of Velcro. Charlotte insisted that the opening was utilitarian. Doc had his doubts. Nevertheless, he added it to the sold pile.

The final item was a dark pink lace teddy. The lace was sort of peek-a-boo and left little to the imagination. It was definitely attention getting and attention holding. Without saying a word, Doc nodded for Charlotte to add it to the sold stack.

"What else, Doc?" Charlotte asked.

"Do you have any colorful crotchless panties?" Doc asked.

"I have royal blue, emerald green, and a perennial favorite, red," Charlotte said.

"What are the damages on the panties?" Doc asked.

"They're only five dollars a pair. If you buy three pair you get a fourth pair for free," Charlotte replied.

"I love a woman that can sell. Put all four pair in the pile and check us out," Doc instructed.

"Has your lust been incited?" Charlotte asked.

"Mine and any other man's who sees her wearing those garments," Doc responded.

"That shows we live up to our name," Charlotte replied.

"No doubt," Marilyn said with a smile.

"We have to get to the Sports Bar and have a quick lunch," Doc said as they exited the boutique.

"Are you famished?" Marilyn inquired.

"You have an appointment for a soak, a body scrub, and a massage at Spa Sereno at 2:00 pm. I promised that you wouldn't keep Paul waiting," Doc explained.

"No, let's not keep Paul waiting," Marilyn replied.

"He's 78 years old and he deserves your respect for his schedule," Doc said with.

Marilyn gave Doc an icy stare. He would eventually swear that he said 28 and not 78.

The couple had a nice but uneventful lunch at the sports bar. They had pleasant conversation between themselves and with some neighbors and local members of the resort.

Marilyn arrived promptly at 2:00 pm for her spa appointment. Doc excused himself and suggested that he would take a nap under a palapa, check out the scenery, work his email, and cruise the internet while he waited.

After a few minutes, Paul entered the spa waiting room and introduced himself. Marilyn was quite taken back by his age and appearance.

Paul led Marilyn into a room containing a large stainless-steel tub of hot, soapy water. He motioned for her to drop her wrap and step into the tub.

Marilyn dropped her wrap and stood slightly ill at ease before Paul. She calmed herself by rationalizing this was purely therapeutic.

After about a half hour, Paul re-entered the room and asked her to step out of the stainless-steel tub. He offered her a towel and invited her into a room across the hall.

This room as referred to as the scrub room. It contained a long table, somewhat resembling a bed with about eight-inch sidewalls, fitted with a hot and cold water supply and a handheld shower. There was a drain at the bottom of the table about six inches below Marilyn's feet.

Paul took Marilyn's towel and invited her to climb onto the scrub table and lay down.

Paul sprayed her naked body with warm water. He took his time starting at the neck and working his way to her feet. After she had been thoroughly drenched, he applied body scrub from her neck to her abdomen and began a gentle exfoliation down to her waistline.

After washing off her check and torso, Paul performed the same task from her waist to her feet. She would tell her close friends that Paul made sure that everything was well scrubbed.

Paul motioned for her to roll over. He repeated the same procedure from the back of her neck to her feet. Upon completion, he helped her into a standing shower in the corner and made sure she was completely rinsed.

He handed her a terrycloth robe and invited her into one of the spa's many massage rooms. He took the robe and motioned for her to lie on the massage table face down.

Doc woke up from his nap beneath the palapa and grabbed his iPhone to check his email. After completing his email, he read a few articles on the newsfeed.

Doc happened to look up and see Marilyn traversing the short distance between the lower clubhouse exit and walking toward him. She was only wearing sexy shoes and a smile. For the first time, she was exercising the option.

"Did I get my money's worth?" Doc asked.

"Yes, and I got your money's worth, too," she replied.

"What do you mean?" Doc asked.

"That hunk soaked, scrubbed, rubbed, and massaged me for two and a half hours," she exclaimed in a slightly higher pitched voice.

"I told them to see that you got some special attention," Doc beamed.

"I got enough extra attention to write a chapter about it in a trashy novel," Marilyn said.

* * *

After experiencing a great lunch at the Sports Bar, a shopping trip at Lust, and a couple hours at Spa Sereno, there was nothing else to do but for the couple to take an afternoon nap.

Doc always told their girls that they were taking a nap. Marilyn would tell them that they were spending some quiet time together. As the girls got older, it was unlikely that they were being fooled.

That night they groomed and dressed for Ladies Night at the nightclub. Doc wore navy dress pants and a blue and white striped shirt. True to her word Marilyn donned a large weave, black, fishnet teddy.

The interesting part about the teddy is that it shaped and formed Marilyn while leaving little to the imagination. She received many complements from the women and a decent number of solicitations from some of the men.

Doc opted for a table contiguous to the dance floor. He said that he wanted to be near the action. Over time he would figure out that a little less action might be better, but that was a lesson he would have to learn.

A thirty-something, petite, Canadian, brunette came to the table carrying two test tube shaped tall shot glasses and introduced herself. She was definitely having a good time at Ladies Night. She straddled Doc's wheelchair seat with ease.

"I'm Stacy. Have you ever enjoyed sex-on-the beach?" she asked.

"Not that I recall," Doc said.

Stacy took one of the two glasses and downed the blue colored liquid inside. She immediately tilted Doc's head backwards and poured the second drink down his throat. Once Doc swallowed, she grabbed his head in her hands and gave him a long, wet kiss.

It took a few years, but Doc later admitted that he almost leaped from the chair and exclaimed, "I'm healed!"

Stacy gave Doc a big huge, a kiss on the left check, and stood up. She walked around the dance floor and returned the glasses to the bar.

"Well . . . wasn't that special?!" Marilyn said with her best Saturday Night Live church lady voice.

"You'll have to tell me later. I can't hear you. The music is too loud," Doc said.

"He's got selective hearing," Marilyn thought to herself. "He doesn't need sex on the beach. He's had it everywhere else over the last ten years," she mused.

A petite blonde approached Doc and Marilyn's table. They had not seen her before. Given the past week's events, they were prepared for just about anything.

"I'm Suzy Randolph. I'm the manager at Spa Sereno," the lady explained.

"We're pleased to meet you," Marilyn replied.

"How was your spa experience?" Suzy asked.

"It was very nice," Marilyn replied.

"Nice! Nice! It got her heart pumping and her blood pounding," Doc exclaimed.

"Paul is known for producing that effect," she replied.

"No doubt," Marilyn said under her breath.

"Come on, tiger. I'll get your heart pounding and your blood pumping," Marilyn offered.

"Not more than when Waver shows up in two days," Doc reminded.

7. To A Mouse (Part I)

It was almost midnight. Doc and Marilyn waited patiently for Waver's plane to arrive and meet her at the baggage carousel. The incoming flight board noted that her flight had arrived, and the passengers were deplaning.

Due to almost blizzard conditions in Minneapolis-St. Paul, Roger had to send Waver a day early. The plan was for her to arrive in the late hours of Saturday night to avoid most of the weekend crowd.

The inclement weather put her at Caliente in the late hours of Friday night. Her arrival would coincide with another rambunctious Saturday and Sunday.

After retrieving Waver's bags, the trio made their way toward the Lincoln Navigator. It wasn't a long distance from baggage claim to the handicap space just outside Tampa International's main terminal.

Just before reaching the vehicle, Wavier exclaimed, "Wait! Wait! I've got to get out of some of these clothes!"

Marilyn and Doc giggled before Doc said, "We know exactly how you feel."

They made the twenty-minute trip from the airport to the resort in record time. The security gate was closed but Doc used his key card to open the tall gate and gain entrance.

It was about five minutes from the gate to 69 Sand Hill Crane Drive. He hoped that it would be uneventful, but at Caliente sometimes things just have a way of happening.

The streets appeared vacant on that early Saturday morning. Just as they turned into Doc's neighborhood, a naked man on a bicycle crossed the intersection in front of the Lincoln.

"He's naked," Waver remarked.

"I think he was wearing a white swimsuit," Doc replied.

"He was naked," Waver repeated.

"I'm pretty sure he was wearing a Speedo. It's a very brief swimsuit," Marilyn said.

"He was naked," Waver said for a third time as they pulled into the garage.

"Why do you think he was naked?" Doc asked.

"He had his ding dong wrapped in some gold rings," Waver said.

Before either Doc or Marilyn could speak, Waver added, "He must be stretching it like some of those African women stretch their necks with rings."

Not wanting to advance the discussion further, the pair got Waver into the house and got her settled. Doc and Marilyn gave each other a knowing look.

Keeping Waver shielded from hundreds of nudists for an entire weekend at the clothing optional resort was going to be much harder than they imagined. They had no idea what was ahead.

*　*　*

Doc's brother, Roger, had given him certain instructions regarding the care and feeding of Waver for the next week. She had certain dietary requirements and needed two prescriptions filled.

The dietary requirements so-called were actually only Waver's dietary preferences. Nevertheless, they were requirements as far as Waver was concerned.

Waver was an early riser and she caught Doc and Marilyn before they could make a quick trip to Walmart for her groceries and medication. It was misting rain outside. The pair believed that the light rain, referred to as liquid sunshine by the locals, would deter Waver from having any encounters before they returned.

Like Robert Burns said in his poem, To A Mouse, "The best laid schemes o' mice an' men oft go awry an' leave us naught but grief an' pain."

Waver bathed, dressed and groomed to greet the day. It wasn't long before Doc and Marilyn's best laid scheme went awry.

The doorbell rang and Waver made her way to the front door. She opened the door and saw a very beautiful young women standing at the door with a briefcase in her hand.

"I'm Claire and I represent LDS," she said.

Waver replied, "Honey, I don't have anything against the Mormons, but I've been a Methodist for over 60 years. You'd have more luck sticking a hot, greased poker up a wildcat's ass than proselyting me."

"I'm not with the Latter-day Saints. I represent the Lifestyle Dating Service," Claire responded.

"Well, I know that my son, David, moved down here to improve himself with the lifestyle. His wife, Marilyn, was supportive and so am I," Waver said.

There was no meeting of the minds between Waver and Claire at that moment. Those trains were running on two different tracks.

"May I come in and talk about Lifestyle Dating Service?" she asked.

"I'm the only single one in this house," Waver said with a chuckle.

"Let's explore some possibilities for you," Claire suggested.

"You can come in and chat, but I doubt you've got a magic wand in that valise," Waver said with a chuckle.

Waver invited her to sit on the large sofa in the living room. It wasn't long before Claire began to tout the benefits of the Lifestyle Dating Service.

"LDS is a social organization. We provide travel assistance to exotic destinations, host monthly social events for our members, and provide a website for our members to arrange dates with other members," Claire explained.

"Well, if I was 20 years younger and single, you might make a sale today," Waver replied.

"You don't have to be younger. We have young men that actually prefer older women. I can have you hooked up with a young, handsome man within 24 hours," Claire boasted.

"How much would that cost?" Waver asked.

"The first month is free. If you like it and want to continue as a member, there's a monthly membership charge," she explained.

"I'm only going to be here a week," Waver said.

"Not a problem. We have affiliated clubs in most large cities," Claire remarked.

"I live in the Minneapolis-St. Paul area. You got any of those hot, young men there?" Waver asked.

After checking her LDS directory, she announced, "We have a large club there. Your trial membership is good while you're here and at any of our affiliated clubs outside Tampa."

"Are there any activities around this week?" Waver asked.

"We have a Sexy Silver party tonight at the Caliente nightclub," Claire responded.

"Sign me up, I don't need a man, but I don't mind a little window shopping," Waver exclaimed.

Within minutes of Claire leaving, Kimberly and Coco ring the doorbell. When she opened the door, she saw two young ladies clad in colorful, very brief wraps. Each of them was holding a tray of Jello shooters.

"How can I help you?" Waver asked.

"We're having an after-party for LDS tonight. Doc said we could put these in his large freezer for later," Kimberly explained.

"Is that Jello?" Waver asked.

"They're called Jello shooters. You just dump them into your mouth," Coco replied.

"Would you like one or two now?" Kimberly inquired.

"I just ate breakfast a few hours ago. Maybe later," Waver said.

The trio made their way to the large kitchen. The young ladies positioned the trays in Doc's freezer. They thanked Waver and she walked to the front door with them to bid the ladies farewell.

Doc and Marilyn had been absent for about two hours and Waver was getting bored. She began rummaging through the house and made her way to the large laundry room.

Waver decided that she would do their laundry. When she removed the first load from the dryer, she quickly noticed that some repair work was needed. It wasn't long until she had taken care of mending some garments.

She heard Doc and Marilyn make their way through the house while calling her name. She appeared in the living room and announced her presence.

"How are you doing, Mom?" Doc inquired.

"Well, it was a busy morning. You had several visitors," she replied.

Doc turned very pale and so did Marilyn. Neither uttered a word before Waver continued her account of events.

"There was a nice LDS girl that showed up and invited me to join. She offered a month's free membership. I accepted and told her I'd come to the next meeting. However, I'm not sure that it'll do me any good," Waver explained.

"That's pretty strange," Marilyn said.

"That's what I thought. Especially with her telling me that they had lots of younger men looking for older women. I may just go up to that Silver Singles party at the nightclub tonight. Just because you look at the menu, you're not obligated to place an order," Waver remarked.

"Mom, that nightclub will be noisy and very crowded. I don't think you'll like it at all," Doc said discouraging Waver.

"I'll see how I feel tonight. If they like older women, I could be like a Twinkie in a room full of fat boys," Waver said.

"Oh my," Marilyn replied.

"Indeed," Doc remarked.

"Two young women stopped by with two trays of Jello for your freezer. They are having a party tonight. They said that you gave them permission," Waver reported.

"I need to sit down," Marilyn said.

"How did that go?" Doc said fearing the answer.

"They were very nice and very polite. They had on a wrap-style dress, but it was obvious that they weren't wearing undergarments," Waver said.

"It's Florida, Waver," Doc explained.

"If those outfits were any shorter, you'd see Christmas," Waver said.

"I need a glass of red wine," Marilyn said.

"I guess you're taking communion early this week," Waver replied slightly sarcastically.

"I'm not sure that I'm going to make it till tomorrow," Marilyn said.

"I did your laundry and saw that you hadn't taken time to do repairs to your undergarments," Waver opined.

"What are you talking about, Waver?" Doc queried.

"She had ripped the seat out of four pair of her panties. I sewed them back together. You'll never know they were ripped. I double stitched all four pair," Waver said.

Realizing that Waver had just sewn the crotch together in the panties she bought from the Lust boutique, Marilyn uttered a muffled, "Thanks."

"Honey you can't put ten pound of feathers in a five-pound bag. You need to buy a size larger," Waver suggested.

"Waver, we got your prescriptions filled. We rushed back to make sure that you take your medicine. We need to go back to grocery shop," Marilyn said.

"I'll be fine here. I'm sure I can find something to get into," she replied.

Doc turned his wheelchair and faced the door. He thought to himself and that's what I'm worried about.

On their drive to the grocery store, it was obvious that she was still fuming about the panty incident. It was more about what Waver said than what she did.

"Ten pounds of feathers, she said! Ten pounds of feathers, my ass," she remarked.

"I think that was her point," Doc replied with some slight humor in his voice.

"Let me tell you something Dr. David Michaels! Those panties have a lot of stretch in them," Marilyn replied with a slightly raised voice.

"Not according to Waver," Doc said tongue-in-cheek.

Before Marilyn could make a reply, her phone rang. She saw that it was Roger, her husband's brother.

"It's Roger. Talk to him. I'm driving," she instructed.

"I'll put him on speaker. He'll get a two for one special," Doc said.

"David, are you enjoying marital bliss?" Marilyn inquired.

"It's raining. Amber has a cold and stomach virus. She's angry that we didn't come to Florida," Roger replied.

"That's what happens when you sleep with nothing but a thin man on top of you," Doc remarked.

"David, that's rude," she responded.

"Speaking of rude . . . how's goes the Waver experience?" Roger asked.

"While we were at the pharmacy, she got a 30-day free membership with the Mormons," Doc reported.

"Mormons! She's a lifelong Methodist, Roger exclaimed.

"It was a local social club with the acronym LDS for Lifestyle Dating Service," Marilyn explained.

"Why did she join?" Roger asked.

"They told her they had younger men looking for older women," Doc said.

"She told me that looking at the menu didn't obligate you to order," Marilyn said with a laugh.

"Was there anything else eventful today?" his brother inquired.

"She sewed the crotch together on four pair of Marilyn's crotchless panties. She thought they were ripped because Marilyn was putting ten pounds of feathers in a five-pound bag," Doc reported.

"You gotta pick that scab. You just have to pick that scab," she remarked.

"That's as much as I can stand to hear right now," Roger remarked.

"Call back in about five or six hours for a Waver update," Doc suggested.

"I will definitely check back," Roger said as he ended the conversation.

"You think my ass is big, don't you?" Marilyn asked.

"I never said that. That's your imagination at work," he replied.

"You keep quoting Waver. What do you really think?" Marilyn implored.

"I'm like Goldilocks at the three bears' house," Doc said.

"What does that mean?" she inquired.

"To paraphrase Goldilocks: It's not too big. It's not too little. It's just right," Doc opined.

"Let's get that medicine and get back. You're about to find the true meaning of 'just right'," she promised.

* * *

It was mid-afternoon and Waver was starting to get hungry. Doc and Marilyn were not back with her groceries. She just needed a snack, so she made her way to the freezer.

Waver opened the freezer door, removed a couple of the barely congealed Jello shooters, and let them slide down her throat. These must be that sugar free Jello she thought. It's got a bite to it.

After overcoming the slight bite of the Vodka in the shooters, she opted for two more shooters. It wasn't until a few minutes later that the special Jello started to have its effect.

Waver roamed around the house for a bit. She decided to take a quick dip in the large, heated, indoor pool. She didn't bring a swimsuit, so she decided to take a skinny dip while no one was there but her.

After about fifteen minutes in the pool, Waver felt the full effects of four Jello shooters. She thought she was a victim of low blood sugar.

While she sat there in a Jello shooters stupor, there was a knock on the front door. On the second round of knocking, the rapping got much louder.

Realizing that answering the door in person would be a chore, Waver loudly yelled, "Come in!" Mako made his way into the pool area and stood silent and surprised.

"I'm Dr. David Michaels' mother, Waver," she said.

"I'm his neighbor, Mako Jenkins," he replied.

"Mako, we have a problem," Waver said.

"How can I help?" Mako asked.

"I had four of those tubes of that diet Jello those two female friends of David's put in the freezer. Instead of boosting my blood sugar, I think they made my blood sugar drop," Waver explained.

"Ms. Michaels, I'm pretty sure that they were Jello shooters made with vodka and Jello. You probably just have a little buzz going," Mako explained.

"What's the cure for that?" Waver asked.

"The easiest cure is to just sit here and let it wear off," Mako suggested.

"I need to ask you one question," Waver implored.

"Ask it," Mako insisted.

"Have you noticed that I'm in my birthday suit?" Waver asked.

"Yes ma'am. I did," Mako said politely.

"Is that a problem?" she asked.

"I think it's great," Mako said.

"Do you belong to that LDS group?" Waver asked.

"As a matter of fact, I do not," Mako replied.

"I have a couple things you need to do for me," Waver instructed.

"Anything," Mako replied.

"Call up at that clubhouse and order us some food – whatever you want, and ham and pineapple pizza for me, and charge it to Dr. David Michaels," she said.

"What else?" Mako asked.

"Then strip off those shorts and shirt and take a skinny dip," she ordered.

Mako shed his clothes faster than the only stripper in a jiggle joint full of Shriners. He folded his clothes and placed them on a nearby patio table.

"I recognize you," Waver remarked.

"I don't remember us meeting. Are you sure?" Mako asked.

"You were naked riding a bicycle near here about 12:30 am this morning," she replied.

"How could you tell that it was me?" Mako asked with a puzzled look.

"I recognize those halos on your schlong," Waver reported.

I've got a question for you, Ms. Michael," Mako said.

"Say on," Waver said.

"Are you going to tell anyone that we went skinny dipping?" Mako asked.

"No, but I may ask a few people if they've heard about it," she replied.

8. To A Mouse (Part II)

It wasn't long before Doc and Marilyn returned with two bags of Waver's favorite groceries. It included some fresh fruit, yogurt, and some odds and ends canned goods.

Doc decided to check the mail. Marilyn opened the front door and made her way into the foyer.

Marilyn looked across the living room to the pool area and into the large screened patio. She screamed and dropped the bags of groceries.

The falling canned goods made quite a crash when they hit the floor. Fresh Florida oranges rolled across the living room and hit the sliding glass doors that separated the two rooms.

Marilyn exclaimed, "Oh Mako! Not Waver!"

"It's not what you think! I can explain this," Mako pleaded.

By this time Doc had rolled through the open door expecting Marilyn to have fallen on the slippery wood floor. When he looked up from the spilled groceries, he noticed a pale-faced Mako sitting naked beside a dazed naked Waver.

"David, he has debauched your mother!" she said accusingly.

"This is a terrible misunderstanding," Mako insisted.

Before Doc could make any sort of reply, Gilbert showed up in the foyer and announced, "Pizza!"

Beverly, Mako's tall sexy blonde wife, stepped out from behind Gilbert. It was obvious that she was unhappy with what she saw.

"So this is your idea of a hot shiksa?" Beverly asked sarcastically.

"They should change your name from Mako to Alley Cat," Marilyn opined.

"I'm telling all of you that this is just a misunderstanding and I can explain what happened," Mako urged.

"Aren't you going to say anything, David?" Marilyn insisted.

"I wasn't aware that Waver had shiksa appeal," Doc remarked.

"I hate to interrupt this neighborly activity, but what should I do with this pizza?" Gilbert inquired.

"Who ordered it?" Doc inquired.

"The ticket says, Mako," Gilbert replied.

"Mako! And on Shabbat no less!" Beverly remarked.

"What type of pizza is it?" Marilyn asked.

"It says ham and pineapple on the receipt," Gilbert replied.

"And pork, too! Oy vey!" Beverly exclaimed.

"Waver made me order it. I don't eat pork. I've never even been tempted by bacon bits on a salad bar!" Mako insisted.

"Gilbert, put the pizza on the dining table. Marilyn, sign the ticket. Mako, tell us what happened," Doc instructed.

"I knocked on the door to tell Marilyn about the monthly book club meeting tomorrow afternoon and extend an invitation from Beverly to her. After the second knock, someone yelled, 'Come in!'" Mako said before taking a deep breath.

"I walked in and Doc's mother was skinny dipping in this pool. She thought she had low blood sugar, but she had finished off four Jello shooters that Kim and Crystal had left in your freezer," Mako said.

"Why did you end up naked in the pool with my mother?" Doc asked.

"She was quite tipsy. She invited me to join her. I figured that that I would stay until the pizza arrived, she ate something, and then revived a little," Mako replied.

"That doesn't explain you engaging in business on the Sabbath," Beverly insisted.

"I conveyed one message from Mrs. Michaels to the sports bar. It was ordered on Doc's account and I have no authority to sign the receipt. Further, I was under a duty to keep this fine lady from injury or death in an alcohol-induced stupor," Mako explained.

"Beverly, could you help Marilyn get Waver out of the pool and to her bedroom?" Doc implored.

Marilyn and Beverly helped a drunken Waver out of the pool and to her bedroom. It was more like propping her up between themselves and letting her drag her feet.

After the three women exited the room, Doc signed Gilbert's receipt and added a very nice gratuity. Gilbert nodded and exited the front door pulling it closed behind him.

Doc immediately burst into uncontrollable laughter at Mako's dilemma. He couldn't resist finding immense humor in the turn of events.

"Doc, this is not funny. This is serious. I was very close to being in a lot of trouble with those two women," Mako said indignantly.

"Hot shiksa," Doc said and again broke into uncontrollable laughter.

Upon returning to the living room, Beverly looked directly at Mako and said, "It's time to leave evald-hathol."

Mako gathered his clothes and walked proudly across the living room floor to the front door. Beverly waved after flashing that cat-that-ate-the-canary expression.

"What did she call him?" Marilyn asked.

"I'm not familiar with a lot of Yiddish but my best guess is old tomcat," Doc replied.

The two had a hearty laugh together. But both cringed when they thought what might happen next when Waver woke up tomorrow.

* * *

Waver woke up late the next morning. She was nursing a pretty good hangover.

"What happened to that shark boy?" she asked at the breakfast table.

"He went home after we put you to bed," Marilyn responded.

"Whew! I thought he'd spent the night and I missed it," Waver remarked.

"It wasn't really pleasant when his wife showed up and saw both of you naked and in the pool together," Doc said.

"She was more upset when Gilbert showed up with a ham and pineapple pizza that you made him order for you," Marilyn said slightly scolding Waver.

"That's not my circus and he's not my monkey," Waver said in a slightly defensive tone.

Attempting to change the subject, Doc asked, "Marilyn are you attending the ladies book club gathering today?"

"It slightly conflicts with your Caliente Fishing Tournament today," Marilyn reported.

"I want to go to the book club meeting. I used to belong to a book club years ago," Waver reported.

"I didn't know you were an avid reader, Waver. What kind of books did you enjoy?" Marilyn inquired.

Before Waver could reply, Doc said, "Trashy romance novels."

"Well, it wasn't as bad as what you and your brother looked at in those dirty books between your mattress and box springs." Waver replied.

"David, I didn't realize you enjoyed pornography," Marilyn said with a smile.

"Actually, they belonged to my brother, Roger. He hid them under my mattress because Waver knew I wasn't into porn," Doc said.

"I couldn't tell who those dirty books really belonged to, so I just ignored it altogether," Waver explained.

"Marilyn, why don't you call Beverly and get the book club moved here. It'll keep Waver from having to travel through the neighborhood," Doc suggested.

"Yes, and we can check on you by cell phone afterwards," she responded.

"Fishing is boring. I'll watch that zombie show and see who gets eaten tonight. I hope it's that smart-assed old woman," Waver said.

"I didn't know you had a part on Fear The Walking Dead," Doc teased.

"My bite is worse than my bark, son." Waver responded.

"Indeed," Doc said under his breath.

* * *

About a dozen ladies began arriving at 4:30 pm for what Doc called the "Dirty Book Club". There were a few familiar faces such as Charlotte, Beverly, Crystal and Kimberly. But most were new to Marilyn.

The ladies seated themselves in the Michaels' spacious den and Marilyn offered several trays of light refreshments and non-alcoholic beverages.

"I hope all of you had the chance to read My Secret Desires by Micki Mitchell. We can give our thoughts and share which of her vignettes we like the best," Beverly instructed.

"What's it about?" Waver asked bluntly.

"It's a collection of fifteen different female sexual fantasies," Beverly replied.

"That's enough to keep me hot in Minneapolis till the spring thaw," Waver said with a laugh.

Marilyn gave a reserved laugh at Waver's remark. The rest of the women thought her observation and commentary was hilarious.

Beverly Jenkins looked around the room to choose her first victim. Her eyes settle on Emily Seals, a forty-something long haired blonde with blue eyes. She looked a lot like a Barbie doll and had the personality to match.

"Emily Seals tell us which fantasy gave you the most excitement," Beverly instructed.

"I really liked the story entitled, 'Trapped In An Elevator,'" Emily replied.

"Tell us about it girl. The title alone warms me up," Waver said loudly.

"According to the book, this middle-aged woman had agreed to pick up and pay for some concert tickets for her college-aged daughter and her fiancé. It was late in the day when she bought the tickets from the ticket office located in the bottom of the athletic complex.

She entered the elevator along with two male athletes. The power failed and they were trapped together," Emily told.

"I know where this is headed," Waver said to Marilyn who put her right index finger across her lips.

Emily continued, "The lady called on the elevator phone. The elevator company told her that there was a general power outage across the city, and it would be at least an hour before they could get assistance to them.

It wasn't long before the elevator got warm and the two young men removed their shirts revealing their toned muscular bodies. They invited the woman to take off her blouse and skirt.

After hesitating, she stripped off her skirt and blouse in the dimly lit elevator. The two college boys stared at her full breasts and long legs."

"How did that make you feel?" Beverly asked.

"It's got me wet," Waver remarked as the other women burst into laughter.

"Waver, you're supposed to be quiet and listen," Marilyn insisted.

Emily continued, "After a bit of coaxing from the two athletes, the lady removed her bra to reveal her large firm breasts and ample nipples. One of them asked to feel her breasts and she nodded.

While she stood on her knees for the young man to caress her breasts, the other young man slowly slipped off her panties."

"Get to the good part," Waver insisted.

"The elevator began to move slowly as the lights came back on. She grabbed her skirt and blouse, slipped them on, waved at the young men, and exited the elevator for the parking lot."

"Damn! That's only PG-13. I was waiting for the hard R version," Waver remarked.

"I think what Ms. Michaels is pointing out is that teasing can be both exciting and frustrating depending upon one's expectations," Beverly said.

"Honey, at my age, you don't waste time before you get to the main attraction," Waver said bluntly.

"Does anyone have a different story that they really enjoyed?" Beverly asked.

"I liked the one called, 'Window Washers,'" Crystal replied.

"Share a brief explanation of the vignette along with your thoughts," Beverly encouraged.

"This lady and her husband live in a luxury condo in a large building in downtown Atlanta. It was a Friday. They had both taken off from work for a three-day sex-a-thon."

"I like where this is headed," Waver whispered to Beverly.

"They were totally nude. The couple began caressing, kissing and fondling each other in the large sunken living room. Suddenly two male window washers positioned their scaffold outside the window.

The woman noticed their presence, but the husband was too excited and engaged to notice," she explained.

"Sounds just like a man," Waver remarked to Marilyn.

"She coaxed her man to lie down on the floor facing away from the window. She mounted him and they began a long love making session. She eventually tumbled off on her back exhausted from the experience.

Although the couple couldn't hear the applause of the window washers, the wife saw their clapping motion and smiles."

"Now that's what I'm talking about. That's why you go for the dirty books instead of just the trashy romance novels," Waver opined.

The room full of ladies laughed and clapped. Marilyn couldn't find a table large enough to crawl under.

* * *

While dirty book club continued, Doc and his sidekick, Mako made their way to the large lake that surrounded the Sand Hill Crane neighborhood on three sides. Mako carried the tackle box and rods while Doc rolled along the asphalt walking path that skirted the lake.

The unnamed lake was great for fishing. However, several alligators and snapping turtles inhabited the lake which deterred any swimmers.

"Now, Doc, we need to talk about yesterday," Mako said.

"I believe I'd let that sleeping dog lie," Doc replied.

"Proverbs 17:5 says, 'He that is glad at calamities shall not go unpunished,'" Mako instructed.

"I was laughing at what Beverly said about you. Your calamity started when Waver yelled, 'Come in!'" Doc said.

"Well, now that we have that straight . . . what's your secret weapon in this fishing tournament?" Mako inquired.

"It's a fishing lure inspired by you," Doc replied.

"Is it the Mako?" he asked excitedly.

"I've named it the Wonder Worm in honor of you," Doc said with a chuckle.

"What makes it so wonderful – other than being inspired by me?" Mako asked.

"It glows in the dark just like your halos on you schmeckle," Doc replied.

"How does that work exactly?" Mako inquired.

"It is a soft, plasticized, PVC, ten-inch worm. Inside are tiny spheres of two chemicals, that when crushed and mixed together, cause a chemically luminescent glow," Doc explained.

"Can you tell me that in plain English?" Mako pleaded.

"When you squeeze the Wonder Worm it lights up," Doc said.

"That's just like the real thing," Mako said with a wide grin.

Doc had enrolled himself and Mako in the tournament earlier in the week. The prizes were $300, $200, and $100, respectively. The winner was determined by the largest fish.

After about a half hour, three college-age girls walked by the anglers and stopped to watch their efforts. They were intrigued since they were unaware that the lake contained any fish.

"Are you having any luck?" one young lady asked.

"We've just gotten started," Doc replied.

"What's your bait?" another girl asked.

"Mako's Wonder Worm. It glows in the dark," Doc said.

"Who's Mako?" the third girl inquired.

"That's me," Mako bragged.

"It really does glow in the dark," the first girl said excitedly as Mako smiled.

As the conversation continued, Mako jerked back his fishing rod to set the hook into a very large fish. It had his rod almost bent double in a few seconds and the line fed off the reel with a fast buzzing sound.

"It's a big one!" Mako exclaimed.

"That's what Waver said at breakfast about yours," Doc said tongue-in-cheek.

"Can we do anything to help?" one of the girls asked.

"According to the tournament rules he has to get it to the bank unassisted, but you can all three grab Mako and keep him from falling into the lake," Doc replied.

After about a ten-minute fight, Mako led the huge fish to the bank and Doc retrieved it. The Wonder Worm was still in its mouth.

Seeing the struggle the tournament judge rounded the lake to where the group had gathered. He carried a small scale and a tape measure.

After examination, the judge declared, "This largemouth bass is 12 pounds and 14 ounces in weight and 19 inches in length. That's a lake record."

"It was caught on Mako's Wonder Worm," Mako exclaimed.

"Noted," the judge replied.

The next day the headline on the Tampa Tribune sports page read, "Mako's Wonder Worm Works!" Of course, we knew that all along . . . .

9. Waver's Day Out

Doc had a morning appointment with Uncle Donald's probate lawyer to handle a few outstanding items and close the estate. Although Doc drove regularly, he had Marilyn take the wheel that morning to navigate the downtown Tampa traffic.

Leaving Waver alone at Caliente was like leaving teenage children alone overnight. You know something's going to happen, but you just can't foresee what it will be. Needless to say, Waver never disappoints.

Once Waver had prepared to greet the day, she turned on the television and began scrolling through the local channels. When she hit Channel seven, she paused to watch the Caliente-related billboards.

The screens generally announced things of local interest or upcoming events. However, one screen held a particular interest for her.

The spa was relocating from the main building to a satellite building closer to Doc's neighborhood. The Grand Opening was set for two days into the future.

Waver heard the doorbell ring followed by three distinctive knocks on the door. She peeked through the curtains and recognized it was Mako.

"Come in!" she blurted out loudly.

Mako gently opened the door, stuck his head inside, and peered around before making his entrance. He was quite cautious.

"I got clothes on," Waver announced.

"So do I," Mako replied.

"Well, you didn't the last time you were here," Waver remarked.

"That's what caused me a world of grief and anguish," Mako said.

"It didn't cause me any. I'm an old woman and I don't worry about upsetting a damn soul," Waver explained.

"No doubt," Mako remarked.

"What do you need?" Waver remarked.

"I came to see if we could borrow Doc's garage tonight for our Texas Hold 'Em night," Mako explained.

"What's wrong with your regular place?" Waver inquired.

"It's being painted, and the painter is leaving his equipment in place until the job is finished," Mako reported.

"You can borrow it under one condition," Waver said.

"What condition would that be?" Mako queried.

"You have to take me to that new spa." Waver replied.

"They've moved and they're not taking any customers for two more days," Mako said.

"If you can't get me an appointment, when Doc and Marilyn get back from the lawyer's office, I'll raise more hell than a jackrabbit in a tin box about any gambling in the garage," Waver promised.

"Let me make a call," Mako said nervously.

"Hello. This is Mako. I need to arrange a full spa treatment for Mrs. Michaels. . . I realize that but this is urgent. Hold on and I'll ask," Mako said.

"What's the question?" Waver inquired.

"What services to you want?" Mako asked.

"I want everything they've got. I want the works," Waver replied.

"Do you want a waxing?" Mako asked.

"If it's part of the works, I'll have one of those too," Waver said confidently.

"You want a man or a woman?" Mako asked

"What do you think?" Waver inquired.

"If I were you, I'd go with a man for the massage and a woman for everything else," Mako recommended.

"Get 'er done," Waver instructed.

"She wants the works including a Brazilian waxing. She wants a man for the massage and a woman for everything else . . . Thanks," Mako said as he terminated the call.

"I'll drive you there in my golf cart. They were doing some staff training, but they'll take you now," Mako reported.

"Let me get my purse," Waver replied.

"You don't need a purse. They'll put it on Doc's bill – even the tip," Mako explained.

"What time are we playing cards tonight?" Waver inquired.

"The game goes from 7:00 pm to 10:00 pm usually. It's shorter occasionally," Mako replied.

"I'll get David to pay for the spa and save my money for gambling," Waver said.

"Hey! You played me. You were going to gamble with the rest of us. This spa thing was just a ruse for your benefit," Mako whined.

"I hope you can read a poker face tonight better than you did this morning," Waver said with a chuckle.

Mako left a note on the foyer table explaining that he had taken Waver to her spa appointment. He reported that she should be finished about 1:00 pm.

* * *

Marilyn and Doc sat in the probate lawyer's waiting room and discussed the situation regarding his mother. They were very worried that their luck would run out and Waver would have a meltdown upon learning that Caliente was a clothing optional resort and complex.

"What do you think about our Waver situation?" Marilyn asked.

"If Roger and Amber don't get back soon, I think our luck is going to run out," Doc said.

"She's like a teenager. When we leave her by herself, she's destined to get into something," Marilyn lamented.

"We've got at least another hour before we get back. You better brace for impact," Doc suggested.

* * *

When the couple returned home, it was obvious that Waver was out on some lark and frolic. Marilyn noticed the note that Mako left on the foyer table. She picked it up and read it with horror.

"Waver's at the spa!" she exclaimed.

"Who said?" Doc inquired.

"Mako's note said that he got her worked in and she's getting the works," Marilyn reported.

"We're not merely fucked. We're most sincerely fucked," Doc remarked.

"There's more," Marilyn replied.

"If I wasn't already seated in this wheelchair, I'd have to find a chair," Doc responded.

"It says that Waver's letting them play Texas Hold 'Em in the garage tonight at 7:00 pm," Marilyn said.

"She plays Texas Hold 'Em a couple days a week at the senior citizens center. She's won the tournament for the last three years. She will empty their pockets tonight," Doc explained.

Marilyn's phone rang. It was Mako reminding them that it was time to pick up Waver at the spa.

"It's brace for impact time. According to Mako, Waver is finished at the spa," Marilyn said.

"You need to drive over in our cart and retrieve her,"
Doc said.

"She's your mother. You go and get her," Marilyn
retorted.

"Let go together. There's strength in numbers," Doc
encouraged.

Waver was waiting near the door of the spa when
Doc and Marilyn arrived. They noticed that she was in
a good mood and quite cheerful to the staff as she bid
them goodbye.

When she climbed into the gold cart, Waver said,
"David, when you get the bill, remember I said it was
worth every penny!"

Marilyn and Doc were dumbfounded. They couldn't
believe that this had turned out well. Unfortunately,
Doc made the mistake that many young lawyers make
in jury trials. He asked one question too many.

"Was there any service you didn't like?" Doc asked.

"I know this is Florida. I know that there's a large
Latin population of wonderful people. But next time
I'm going with an American," Waver said.

"What are you talking about Waver?" Doc answered.

"That woman took me from carpet to hardwood in
about ten minutes and even pulled up the weeds
around the backdoor. Mako recommended that
Brazilian lady, but next time I'm sticking with
Americans," Waver explained.

When they arrived back at the house, Mako was
there to ensure that Waver was fine, and that Doc

understood the Texas Hold 'Em game was on for the night.

"How was your time at the spa?" Mako asked.

Standing behind Waver, Doc and Marilyn waved their arms wildly and made gestures for Mako to not ask questions. Unfortunately, they were both too late.

"It was a very pleasant experience. But the next time we take a skinny dip, you won't recognize me," Waver said as she made her way into the house.

"What's she talking about?" Mako asked.

"I guess you think it's funny, don't you?" Marilyn asked.

"Funny? What am I supposed to think is funny?" Mako asked excitedly.

"Arranging for Waver to get a Brazilian," Marilyn retorted as she walked into the house.

"She wanted the works. She said she wanted everything that Marilyn got. She wanted a waxing," Mako tried to explain to Doc.

"She meant to remove a few facial hairs," Doc said.

"How was I to know that? Nobody told me that," Mako whined.

"Did she yell, 'Come in?'" Doc inquired.

"Yes, but I was . . ." Mako tried to explain before Doc interrupted him.

"That was your mistake last time. That was your mistake this time. You just won't learn," Doc remarked as he rolled through the front door and closed it behind him.

"Oy Vey," Mako remarked shaking his head in disbelief.

* * *

Later that day, Mako passed Waver walking to the mailbox to mail a few postcards to her Minneapolis friends. When she saw it was him, she waved to get him to stop his golf cart. He realized that it wasn't the thing to do but he didn't want to be rude.

"Ever since you turned that Brazilian woman loose on me, I've been a nervous wreck. There's a bit of soreness where she pulled up the carpet, too." Waver remarked.

"Now Miss Waver, I didn't realize . . ." Mako started before Waver interrupted.

"I'm not blaming anything on you. I should have asked a few more questions. It's my fault. I stopped you because I want to ask you about herbal remedies – ointments, creams, oils, etc.," Waver explained.

"I've not tried it myself, but there's a lady down the street that uses CBD oil in some edibles. It apparently calms you down. I don't know if it would have any topical relief for your . . . er, . . uh . . . condition," Mako replied.

"See if we can buy some from her," Waver suggested.

"I check on it and be right back," Mako said.

In a few minutes Mako returned with a small bottle of oil for Waver. She thanked him profusely.

"Did she give you any instructions?" Waver asked.

"She said it was mint flavored. You just put a few drops under your tongue, and it'll work almost immediately," Mako explained.

"There can't be anything to it. There are not more than a few drops in this little vial," Waver remarked.

"I'm just telling you what she said," Mako disclaimed.

"I'll take some now. It's only an hour or so till the card game," Waver replied.

"Do you need anything else?" Mako inquired.

"How much do I owe you?" Waver inquired.

"She said she'd take it up with Doc," Mako replied.

As soon as Mako drove away, Waver took the top off the small vial. She opened her mouth, lifted her tongue, and squirted its contents evenly beneath her tongue. She tossed the vial into the trash as she walked through the garage and into the house.

At a little before 7:00 pm the Texas Hold 'Em gang began arriving at the Michaels' garage. It was a larger than normal number of participants.

"Better go get Waver. The gambling is about to begin," Doc instructed Marilyn.

Marilyn returned with Waver and helped her get seated at the table. Waver was unusually happy and quite laid back.

"It must be her version of poker face. She's very mellow," Doc remarked.

"When I went to tell her that the poker gang was here, she said, 'Thank you, baby,'" Marilyn replied.

Mako appeared at one of the open garage doors and asked, "How's Waver?"

"Why do you ask?" Doc queried.

"She flagged me down today and was complaining that the spa experience had made her a nervous wreck and that she was suffering some discomfort from the Brazilian," Mako replied.

"You better always let her think that the Brazilian was the wax technician and not the type of waxing," Marilyn remarked.

"She wasn't upset with me. In fact, I helped her with her problems," Mako beamed.

"What type of help did you provide?" Doc inquired.

"I got her some CBD oil from your neighbor," Mako explained.

"Oh, Mako! You've doped up poor Waver!" Marilyn said with incredulity. "You are banned from this house as long as Waver is here," Marilyn exclaimed.

"Why? I mean, I was trying to help . . . and . . . she was appreciative," Mako stammered.

"It is obvious that she casts some sort of spell over you and your mind stops working. Once she has you in her clutches, you'll willingly do her bidding," Doc scolded.

"If she loses her pension money tonight, you're on the hook," Marilyn charged.

"It's a $100 nightly limit. I'm safe," Mako said with a sigh.

"You're safe until I tell Beverly what you have done," Marilyn scolded.

"Now we don't have to bring Beverly into this. She'll get overly excited if it involves Waver," Mako insisted.

"Mako, if you're playing, find yourself a seat," Dave McDonald insisted.

"Deal 'em boys. I'm making you my bitches tonight," Waver said loudly.

"This is your doing!" Doc said into Mako's left ear.

Waver did an ante of the $20 maximum. One of the six players folded but the remaining five looked determined.

As the dealer turned the first three community cards, Waver started a slightly annoying chant of, "Flop! Flop! Flop!"

The flop turned over a king and two queens. It was a little early to say if it was a good flop or bad flop.

When the bets and raises were in, Waver had $50 in chips on the line. As the dealer started to show the fourth community card, Waver began singing from the Byrds 1960s hit, "Turn, Turn, Turn:"

> 'To everything (turn, turn, turn),
> There is a season (turn, turn, turn)'

The fourth or turn card revealed a two. It was only advantageous if you were holding a couple of twos.

When it came Waver's turn to bet, she proclaimed, "I'm goin' to the river. I'm all in!"

Before shoving her chips forward, Dave McDonald reached to stop her. Waver wasn't happy with his actions, but Mako's Magic Elixir kept her from having a Waver tantrum.

"Ms. Michaels, if you go all in, I'm going to spank your ass with my hand," Dave McDonald said.

"Well, it won't hurt any worse than when that Brazilian woman pulled up my crab grass. . . All in!" she replied as she shoved her chips forward for a second time.

All the players were out but Waver, Dave McDonald, Mako, and Charlotte. The last community card, called the river card, turned up a deuce.

Mako only had two eights plus the two queens from the community cards. Charlotte had a pair of sevens plus the pair of queens from the community cards. Dave flipped his cards to reveal a hand of three kings plus the two queens. It was a full house.

"Winning full house, Waver," Dave exclaimed as he reached for the pot.

"Four deuces, bitch." Waver exclaimed.

"Ya'll keep playing. I'm headed inside to watch that zombie show. I'm praying those walkers get that old bitch tonight," Waver said as she gathered up her winnings.

"Can you believe that?" Charlotte asked.

"Never underestimate the power of Mako's Magic Elixir," Doc said tongue-in-cheek.

10. Run & Fun

One undeniable fact about Caliente Resort is that there are regular activities and special events. The regular activities are weekly or monthly, but special events take place only a few times yearly.

Today presented the Dare to Bare 5K Run, a special annual event, in the afternoon and a monthly foam and pool party all day long. Doc and Marilyn had plans for both, but they had to find a way to pacify Waver for the day. Sometimes fate supplies the answers to our problems.

At 7:30 am Doc's phone began playing its 1950s style rotary telephone ring tone. They knew immediately that it was Roger.

"Good morning, Roger," Doc said trying to hide the fact that he was awakened by the call.

"We're at the Tampa airport and we're headed your way," Roger explained.

"That's great but why did you cut your honeymoon short?" Doc inquired.

"Apparently we picked the monsoon season to spend a week in Hawaii and Amber is still having some problems," Roger replied.

"Are you ready to receive visitors later this afternoon?" Roger asked.

"We'll have the goats milked by then," Doc replied.

"We're going to grab a quick breakfast and spend the day at the beach," Roger informed his brother.

"We feasted on hot biscuits, country ham, and red eye gravy. You should have gotten here sooner," Doc chided.

"We'll get some breakfast at McDonalds," Roger replied smugly.

"Better shop Hardees if you want country ham. McDonalds can only offer you bacon, sausage, or steak," Doc retorted.

"Later," Roger said as he terminated the call.

Marilyn and Doc celebrated with glee. They saw this as an opportunity to send Waver back to Minnesota a few days early.

"You better get ready. The Dare to Bare 5K starts at 9:00 am," Marilyn urged.

"What about Waver?" Doc asked.

"She had a big day yesterday. I'll get her up at 8:30 am and tell her Roger and Amber will arrive late afternoon," Marilyn replied.

"Meet me at the finish line at about 10:30 am. After the race, we can spend a few hours at the foam and pool party.

"I'll give Waver the remote and let her catch up on her Netflix Originals," Marilyn promised.

While Doc showered, shaved, and dressed, he giggled about the prospect of winning the Dare to Bare 5K. Unknown to Caliente, wheelchairs usually win most marathons and even 5K and 10K runs due to the speed disparity between a racing wheelchair and human legs.

Wheelchairs can't compete in 100-meter and 400-meter runs but they top most of the longer races. In fact, wheelchair participants are usually placed in a separate category in marathons.

* * *

When Doc arrived at the starting point of the 5K racecourse he was met by his sponsor, Dave McDonald of Dave's Marina. He was excited because of the publicity generated by the first ever wheelchair entry in the Dare to Bare 5K event.

"Doc, you are enrolled in the regular category and the special wheelchair category that was created just for you," Dave said excitedly.

"So, if I win either category, you'll be happy?" Doc asked.

"What do you mean 'if'? You're the only contestant in the wheelchair category. All you have to do is cross the finish line and we're winners," Dave exclaimed.

"I better lose this shirt and shorts, or I'll be disqualified," Doc said.

"Good idea. I'll get one of the water girls to help you," he replied.

Actually, two water girls showed up to quick strip Doc. A hot blonde grabbed his shirt and a hot brunette jerked off his shorts.

"Have you ever been stripped by two women before?" the blonde asked.

"Not at the same time," Doc replied.

"Let's get to the starting line," Dave urged.

With the runners in position, the judge fired a flare pistol to signal the start of the race.

Although the course wound through the campus, it was tabletop flat and all of it was paved. It wasn't long before Doc had broken out of the pack and held a substantial lead.

With about 1,000 meters to go, it was obvious to Steve Riley and the crowd that Doc was going to take the race. The crowd was more subdued that in past races. It wasn't that a wheelchair would win the race, but that it was going to win by as much as 200 meters.

Doc crossed the finish line at breakneck speed. All but about ten runners walked off the track. One petite thirty something female runner crossed the finish line several minutes after Doc.

Steve Riley gave Doc a congratulatory handshake and asked to speak with him privately before the results were announced. Doc nodded and rolled away from the hearing of the attendees.

"Doc, we're really happy for you. But if a wheelchair always wins this race the number of able-bodied contestants will diminish and this will become basically a wheelchair race," Steve said somberly.

"Most races keep wheelchair contestants in a separate category apart from regular contestants. Normal runners can't compete with a wheelchair in marathon or near marathon races," Doc explained.

"Is there anything that we can do about this year's race without being unfair to you and Dave's Marina?" Steve asked.

"Did Dave pay one entrance fee or two?" Doc asked.

"He paid only one," Steve replied.

"Declare that I only competed in the wheelchair category and declare the second person to cross the finish line to be the non-wheelchair winner," Doc suggested.

"Dave McDonald will be livid," Steve replied.

"He didn't pay two entrance fees so it's his fault. But next year require wheelchairs to compete in only the wheelchair category," Doc said.

"Good idea," Steve responded.

"One more thing," Doc said.

"What is that, Doc?" Steve asked.

"If you tell anyone about this, I will tell everyone here that you wear women's panties under your dress slacks," Doc threatened.

Steve placed his right index finger across his lips and then made a large X across his chest. Doc nodded approvingly.

When the standings were announced and the winners named, everyone was happy but Dave McDonald. He was quite sad that he had not paid two entrance fees.

"Doc, I am so sorry that I screwed this up," Dave said sadly.

"We won! How can you be unhappy?" Doc inquired.

"We should be carrying home both prize checks and two trophies," Dave lamented.

"My grandfather used to say, 'Pigs get fat and hogs get slaughtered.' Keep that in mind," Doc urged.

"Is there anything else I can do for you today?" Dave asked.

"Yes, get those two water girls to bring my clothes and get them back on me. I don't want Waver meeting me at the front door like this," Doc said with wide eyes.

"No problem and I'll see you at the foam party a little later," Dave replied.

About the time Marilyn arrived at the Tiki Bar two of the water girls were assisting him to get dressed. It was quite helpful but unnecessary.

"At least they're helping you get dressed rather than undressed," Marilyn remarked.

"They helped with that at the starting line," Doc replied.

Dave McDonald approached the couple with a sad look and said, "Doc won both races, but I forgot to pay the entrance fee for the second race. He lost the main race by default but won the wheelchair division."

"He got what he wanted the most," Marilyn remarked.

"What was that?" Dave asked.

"Two water girls undressing and then dressing me," Doc remarked.

Ignoring Doc's remark, Marilyn asked, "So how does this foam party work?"

"The resort will use a blower full of bubble juice and fill that eight foot by twelve foot by four-foot deep transparent plastic area with foam. Then you get in and move around like you are in a big bubble bath," Dave McDonald explained.

"What's the point?" Doc asked.

"To be or not to be," Dave said somewhat cryptically.

Marilyn inquired, "To be or not to be what?"

"Groped," Dave said with a laugh.

"Oh! OK," Marilyn replied with eyes opened wide.

"When the whistle blows jump in. I'll see that you don't get molested," Doc promised.

Marilyn walked to the gate and stood in line to get into the foam container. She was wearing a small, orange bikini.

"I'll buy you a ginger ale if that suit lasts more than five minutes," Dave McDonald remarked.

"That appears to be a safe bet – for you," Doc replied.

Once the first round of the foam party commenced, all you could really see were lots of arms, legs, heads, and bottoms. Swimsuit tops and bottoms were flying in every direction.

After about 15 minutes the security guy blew his whistle for the revelers to get out. Another set of about 25 participants filed into the foam tank and the party began for a second time.

"I don't know what happened to my swimsuit," Marilyn remarked covered with foam.

"I'm sure it went to some needy person," Dave said.

"Go rinse off in that outdoor shower before you get into any more trouble," Doc said with a chuckle.

Doc rolled toward the eight outdoor showers. There were four large shower stalls enclosed on three sides. Each stall contained back to back shower heads and controls. The front was open.

Marilyn stepped into one of the units and began to rinse off. It wasn't long before all the outdoor showers were full, and a line formed nearby.

After Marilyn exited the shower and wrapped a towel around her, she whispered to Doc, "I got groped."

"A little or a lot?" Doc inquired.

"Less than on a date with you," she replied curtly.

"Indeed," Doc remarked.

As they made their way to the handicapped gate just beyond the outdoor showers, they heard someone yelling, "Doc! Doc!" When Doc and Marilyn turned, they saw it was Steve Riley.

"Doc, next Sunday is your Birthday Bash," Steve explained.

"Steve, you have been given bad information. My birthday is two months away," Doc said.

"Doc, next month is your birthday. None of the folks here know the date of your real birthday. It's going to be the theme for next Sunday's frivolities," Steve said.

"You are using Doc's bogus birthday as an excuse to party?" Marilyn asked.

"I didn't think you needed an excuse to party at Caliente," Doc said with a chuckle.

"Come on Doc," Steve whined.

"Will there be presents?" Doc asked bluntly.

"They'll be games and prizes, a live band, free cake and hot dogs for the first 100 guests, and you and Marilyn will have free food and drink all day long," Steve explained.

"I'll provide the birthday sex for you afterwards. You know – like the song Birthday Sex by Jeremih," Marilyn reported.

"Steve, do you realize that next Sunday is Doc's birthday?" Doc asked with a smile.

"I just heard that," Steve responded.

* * *

When Doc and Marilyn returned to the house, they noticed an unfamiliar car in the driveway. Doc believed it was a rental car that Roger and Amber drove from Tampa International to the house.

Doc opened the door and rolled inside. His brother, Roger, and his sister-in-law Amber stood to greet him.

After exchanging pleasantries, Doc inquired, "Where's Waver?"

"She's in the den getting a cut and color from Chris Jones," Amber explained.

"Does she have plans?" Marilyn asked.

"Let's hope not," Doc said.

"David, we have two important things to tell you," Roger said solemnly.

"Let's hear it," Doc replied.

"First, Amber is pregnant. That explains her morning sickness in Hawaii. We tried an early pregnancy test (EPT) and it showed positive," Roger said.

"What's the second important thing?" Marilyn queried.

"We've decided to buy a house and move to Tampa," Roger said.

"We can't leave Waver alone in Minneapolis," Doc exclaimed.

In a minute or so Waver entered the room and said, "I've got an announcement to make."

"Say on, Waver. I doubt you can shock us," Roger responded.

"I've decided to sell my house in Minneapolis and move to Tampa," Waver announced.

Trying to maintain his composure, Doc asked, "What part of Tampa are you considering?"

"I'm going to find a condo or villa at this resort and move," Waver said.

"That's wonderful! We're buying a house at this resort, too!" Amber said.

Trying to change the subject, Doc announced, "Amber's pregnant!"

"I knew that," Waver replied.

"How did you know?" Amber asked.

"I heard Roger tell David just a few minutes ago," Waver explained.

"Pop a cork, Marilyn! It's time to introduce Dom Perignon to the family," Doc said with incredulity.

"I'll take ginger ale or diet soda. My champagne days are on hold for the next several months," Amber remarked.

"The celebration may be a bit premature," Roger explained.

"We have to sell our house and find one here. I have to transfer my practice here. I've got to give notice to the Vikings organization," Roger said.

"How long will all that take?" Marilyn asked.

"At least six months maybe nine," Roger said.

"What's your time frame Waver?" Doc inquired.

"I have to sell my place and find a villa or ground floor condo here. I think at least six months too," Waver reported.

Doc and Marilyn looked at each other with an approving glance.

"You should get your things out of the car for the evening here," Doc recommended.

"Actually, we're got reservations for two days in Orlando at one of the Disney hotels. We've got a room for Waver, too," Amber said.

"Why do I have a room?" Waver asked.

"You've got a hot date tomorrow with Mickey Mouse," Roger replied.

"I doubt he's better than Mako," Waver remarked.

"Who is Mako?" Roger asked.

"Long story for another time," Doc said.

11. Baseball & Birthdays

A nearby bolt of lightning followed by a very loud crash of thunder put an end to Marilyn's morning beauty sleep. She sat up in the king size bed, looked out the window, and noticed that a moderate amount of rain had started falling.

Doc had been awake for an hour or so. He was working through his email and reading the newsfeed on his laptop computer.

"Are you excited about your birthday bash?" Marilyn asked.

"Only about half as excited as I'm going to be when I get this computer turned off and get you turned on," Doc replied.

Doc exited the program, set aside the laptop, and turned to hug his wife. It was at that point the he heard a tapping on the back-bedroom door.

"Go see who it is," Doc said.

"I'm naked!" Marilyn explained.

"It's March 1st so it's not Santa. You won't make the naughty list yet," Doc remarked.

Marilyn went to the door and peered through the sheers. She recognized a familiar face.

"Well, who is it?" Doc insisted.

"It's Mako," Marilyn replied.

"Let him in," Doc said with a sigh.

"Happy Birthday, Doc!" Mako exclaimed.

"We're all in our birthday suits, too," Doc exclaimed slightly mocking Mako.

"Can I spank you?" Mako joked.

"With your reputation, you're not getting anywhere *near* my bare ass," Doc insisted.

"David, that's just rude," Marilyn rebuked.

"It's Ok. He'll mellow out during the baseball game," Mako responded.

"What baseball game?" Doc inquired.

"It's what I've been trying to tell you. The Tampa Bay Rays are playing the Baltimore Orioles in the first exhibition game this year," Mako said.

"Why should I be excited about this?" Doc queried.

"There's a big party at the Sports Bar at 1:00 pm for watching it on the local cable channel. It's fifty cent draft beer, dollar hotdogs, and lots of free prizes," Mako explained. It's the warmup for your birthday bash at 4:00 o'clock," Mako explained.

"We'll be there," Marilyn promised.

"Wear panties, a bikini, or really short shorts, and a crop top," Mako suggested.

"I don't have a crop top," Marilyn replied.

"Bring me one of your knit tops and a pair of scissors," Mako instructed.

Marilyn went scurrying off to do as Mako requested. She thought that she'd probably wear a white thong bikini.

"Mako, your skill sets, and persuasive charms never cease to amaze me," Doc said.

"Why do you say that?" Mako inquired.

"You knock on my bedroom door, block me from marital relations, roll my naked wife out of bed, and send her scurrying for a t-shirt and a pair of scissors so you can slut her up for a Caliente Baseball Bash," Doc explained.

"It's my sincerity," Mako replied.

"No doubt," Doc said under his breath.

Marilyn returned wearing a tight fitting royal blue t-shirt. Her bottom was still bare.

Mako took the scissors and cropped the t-shirt just where the bottom twenty percent of her breasts would show. He motioned for her to lean to the side and there was even a better show.

"Go put on some bottoms," Mako instructed.

As Marilyn scurried away for her thong, Doc said, "This is truly an eventful day."

"Why do you say that?" Mako asked.

"You have asked a woman to put *on* clothes instead of trying to get them off," Doc replied.

Marilyn returned wearing the navy crop top and the white thong. It was provocative – even for a Caliente Sunday. She gave a slow 360-degree spin for effect.

"What do you think?" she asked.

"It looks great, absolutely great," Mako said.

"There's no hail damage either," Doc added.

"I'll see you there a little before 1:00 pm," Mako said.

"Are there any further instructions from our neighborhood fashion designer?" Doc asked.

"You may resume your normal Sunday morning marital relations," Mako replied as he exited the back door.

"Did you tell him that we were making love?" Marilyn asked.

"No, I did not," Doc replied sternly.

"How did he know?" Marilyn asked.

"He's got a sixth sense about that sort of thing. He can read your aura," Doc suggested.

"Can you read my aura?" Marilyn inquired.

"No, but I can tell your future," Doc replied.

"And I can tell yours," Marilyn responded as she crawled into bed and pulled up the covers.

* * *

Doc and Marilyn arrived at Calypso Cantina at 12:45 pm and the bar was already at about two-thirds capacity. It seemed like a lot of excitement for a pre-season baseball game.

A tall, thin gentleman walked to where Doc and Marilyn were seated and said, "I'm Shorty Jones. I'm hosting this shindig for the resort."

"I'm Marilyn and this is my husband, Dr. David Michaels," she replied.

Doc stretched out his right arm to shorty and said, "Just call me Doc."

"I hope I'm not being too nosy but you're well over 6 feet tall. How is it that your name is Shorty?" Marilyn inquired.

"In college I played shortstop for on the University of South Florida baseball team. That gave rise to my nickname," Shorty Jones explained.

"What should we expect today?" Doc asked.

"Every time that Tampa Bay makes a hit, we draw for a prize. We'll give a numbered ticket to every lady here. Men are not eligible for prizes," Shorty explained.

"I like this party!" Marilyn exclaimed.

"Doc will like it, too," Shorty said with a smile.

Every able-bodied customer stood as the national anthem was played. They all waited excitedly for the first pitch.

There were no hits by the Baltimore Orioles and no runs scored. When Tampa Bay went to bat, the lead-off batter doubled, and the Rays had a man on base.

"Number 321" Shorty yelled.

"That's the number on my ticket!" Marilyn said with excitement.

"Spin around and jump up a few times. Show us how excited you are," Shorty insisted.

Marilyn followed Shorty's instructions to the letter. The crowd yelled, clapped, and whistled as much as if the Rays batter had hit a homerun. Needless to say Doc understood the need for the peek-a-boo crop top.

Shorty handed Marilyn a Rays logo and colored thong and a matching Tampa Devil Rays visor. She put on the visor but held onto the new thong.

It was a busy afternoon at the Caliente Baseball Bash. By the end of the game, the Rays had scored 10 runs on 11 hits with the Orioles scoring 5 runs on 7 hits. The audience was happy about the result but were happier about momentarily viewing two dozen bare breasts on that early Sunday afternoon.

At the end of the baseball game, Shorty came over to speak to Doc and Marilyn. She was wearing her Rays visor and waving her matching thong.

"Do you do this for every Tampa Bay Devil Rays baseball game?" Doc asked.

"We do it for the first exhibition game, the first game of the regular season, and any playoff games involving Tampa Bay," Shorty explained.

"I really like it. I wish it was every week," Marilyn replied.

"In the fall we have a football party for every Tampa Bay Buccaneers game and have the prize drawings at halftime," Shorty added.

"I'm the newest Tampa Bay Buccaneers fan," Marilyn announced.

"I'll see you at Doc's Birthday Bash at 4:00 pm at the Tiki Bar," Shorty promised.

"We'll be there," Doc replied.

In a few minutes DJ Nick Colorado appeared at the Michaels' table. Doc indicated for him to be seated.

"I wanted to talk to you about Doc's Birthday Bash. I didn't have your email address so I couldn't add you to the newsletter or send you a copy of the graphic," Nick said.

"What did we miss?" Doc asked.

"We've named the event 'Doc's Sluts-R-Us Birthday Bash' and encouraged the women to wear their sexiest resort wear," Nick explained.

"I've got to rush home and change," Marilyn said as she stood and left the table.

"I guess she heard all she needed," Doc remarked.

"There's not much more. We will play music, offer food and beverages from the bar, play games with prizes, and have some contests. We have a gift for every lady present, too," Nick said.

"What is that – a kiss from Doc?" Doc asked with a chuckle.

"Actually it's a set of non-pierced nipple jewelry," Nick responded.

"How does that work?" Doc inquired.

"It's similar to regular nipple jewelry except it's held in place by small rubber bands around the nipples. It like the ones that orthodontists use," Nick explained.

"I'm familiar with those," Doc replied.

"The nipples or the jewelry?" Nick asked with a smile.

"The small rubber bands," Doc said.

"I'm heading down to help finish with the decorations and set up my equipment," Nick said.

"We'll be there a few minutes before 4:00 pm. How long does it last?" Doc asked.

"Until we roll out the last drunk or by 9:00 pm, whichever comes first," Nick replied.

Marilyn returned clad in a rich, royal blue translucent mini dress with matching blue heels with sparkles. She had on darker blue and silver jewelry.

The dress was more opaque in its long sleeves and much less so across the chest and torso. It held everything in place, but it left little to the imagination.

"Are you trying to win the Sluts-R-Us competition?" Doc queried.

"I'll take win, place, or show," Marilyn retorted.

"Has the rain stopped?" Doc asked.

"It's very light. We need to make our way to the Tiki Bar in case it gets heavier," Marilyn opined.

At the Tiki Bar, DJ Nick was playing oldies. He told patrons that it was for the 'oldie' that was a year older. In response, Doc quoted from the Toby Keith song, "Good As I Once Was:"

"I ain't as good as I once was, but I'm as good once, as I ever was."

The place was decorated with large colorful balloons and crepe paper streamers. There was a large banner that read: Sluts-R-Us.

There was a birthday cake large enough to feed a hundred people. It was brightly decorated with one huge white candle in the very center of the cake.

Every lady got one free domestic draft beer coupon when they entered the place. It was paid open bar for everything else. They were also recipients of a nice set of non-pierced nipple jewelry.

After about a half hour of music, dancing, and socializing, Nick called for the first party game. He called it the Blow My Candle game. It was supposed to identify the person who could best blow Doc's candle. The competition was limited to the first dozen attendees to volunteer.

Ten females and two males were given white balloons to inflate. The two men were given trick balloons that would automatically burst when they reached a certain size. The group had one minute to inflate their balloon as large as possible without causing it to burst.

The two males lasted only about 15 seconds. One cried foul but got little sympathy from the audience. At the end of the competition, there were only three participants remaining.

DJ Nick faked being able to decide which lady had the largest balloon. He told them that the person who could release her balloon and have it land nearest Doc would win the prize.

As the balloons raced toward Doc, two flew out the Tiki Bar windows and the third landed in Doc's lap. It belonged to a delightfully personable redhead who earned a $20 Caliente gift card and ended up in Doc's lap for a couple of songs.

At the end of a few songs, Nick declared it was time to play a game called Is It Her? Doc was immediately blindfolded before the game was explained.

"I'm told that Doc and Marilyn have been married for several years. The purpose of this game is to determine whether he can identify her in a crowd. We need a dozen volunteers plus Marilyn to stand in this line and prepare for Doc to give a totally unnecessary breast exam while blindfolded, Nick explained.

"Oh hell!" Doc said loudly.

"There's more. If Doc is unable to identify Marilyn correctly, everyone in the line gets 20 percent discount coupon on a single spa service.

But, if Doc can correctly identify Marilyn from the lineup, there's a free couples day pass, to use or give to your friends, plus the 20 percent coupon," Nick explained.

After giving a quick, but careful, check of three or four of the ladies, Doc blurted out, "That's Crystal!"

The crowd broke into laughter and cheers. Crystal became very red faced when her boyfriend inquired how Doc was able to make her identification.

After a few more tries, Doc exclaimed, "That's her. That's Marilyn!"

The crowed clapped and cheered and the ladies who participated in the contest were very pleased with the prizes.

"By the way, how were you able to identify Crystal's boobs?" Marilyn inquired.

142

DJ Nick tinked, tinked, his wine glass to let me know it was Crystal. It was pre-planned, but it went over well," Doc admitted.

"Did he signal you when it was me?" Marilyn quipped.

"It's like the scientific method. I applied years of experimentation and observation, dear," Doc said tongue-in-cheek.

Marilyn tended to believe Doc's account. However, there was a bit of her that believed that he and DJ Nick had employed some covert identification method.

As the party approached 8:30 there were two contests remaining. The bar and food traffic had slowed. DJ Nick decided to run the Best Breasts and Sexiest Outfit contests simultaneously.

"We know that most of you birthday revelers are either traveling or working tomorrow. Consequently, we're running the next contests simultaneously.

We need anyone that wants to compete in the Best Breast, Sexiest Outfit, or both contests to line up across this back wall," he instructed.

There were twenty ladies that formed a line across the back wall. It included blondes, brunettes, redheads, and a few with silver hair.

"Ok. We've asked our general manager, Steve Riley to pick the sexiest outfit winner. The winner will receive a $50 Caliente cash card. The rest of the contestants will receive a free wine or mixed drink coupon. After that, we'll let applause decide the winner of the Best Breasts competition," Nick explained.

Steve Riley looked carefully at the outfit on each lady. He even had them make a 360 degree turn so he could view the rear of each lady. He narrowed the field to two ladies.

One was wearing a sheer red teddy with red high heels. The other one was wearing a naughty school-girl halter and very, very short plaid skirt.

"I've looked and looked but I just can't decide. So . . . I've decided to award a $50 Caliente cash card to both of these beautiful ladies," Steve Riley announced.

His decision was a clear crowd pleaser but picking two ladies was likely his design from the beginning. Additionally, most customers, including the contestants, recognized that the outfits, not the ladies, were the criteria.

"If you don't intend to be in the Best Breasts Competition, we ask you to step out of the line at this time," Nick announced.

No one stepped out of the line. All twenty ladies were permitted to compete.

Nick made his way down the line of ladies and used the audiometer application on his smart phone to measure the crowd response noise level.

After the first pass, he narrowed the competition to three contestants. As he got ready for the finals, he acted as though his phone audiometer simply wouldn't work. He beat it against his hand a few times and then walked over and had a brief conversation with Steve Riley.

"It appears that Nick is experiencing technical difficulty with his cell phone. It seems the only logical thing to do is award a breakfast for two at Café Ole to each of these three ladies," Steve announced.

Even though most folks realized that this was probably pre-planned, it was really good public relations for the resort.

Marilyn happened to be one of the finalists in Best Breasts competition. From that day forward Doc regularly referred to her as Miss Tittie.

The name stuck with them and it wasn't long before a lot of their friends knew her as Miss Tittie rather than Marilyn.

12. Block Party

One of the traditions at Caliente Resort was the rotation of the annual block parties so that there would be one every month of the year. Each block had a theme for their party. Some block parties were naughty, and others were naughtier.

This year the Sand Hill Crane neighborhood had planned for a costume party. There was no particular theme. You could come as anything or anyone. You could even come in your real birthday suit!

"What's your costume for Tuesday's party going to be?" Marilyn asked.

"I'm going with my U.S. Army Ranger outfit complete with vest, knee pads, and an air pistol in my holster," Doc replied.

"Do you think carrying a weapon is wise?" she inquired.

"It's an air pistol. Lest anyone complain, I'll remove the clip and CO_2 cartridge," Doc said.

"What's your costume?" Doc asked.

"I'm going with a body painted costume of Wonder Woman," she replied.

"Who's doing that?" Doc queried.

"Randy Anderson, the spray tanning guy," she replied.

"Can I watch?" Doc asked.

"You might end up with a pistol in your pocket," she advised.

"It won't be the first time," Doc responded.

"It takes that spray a while to dry. Let's head over to Randy's. I've got a 3:00 pm appointment and the party starts at 6:00 pm," Marilyn suggested.

Randy lived about two blocks from the Michaels' in one of the two-bedroom villas. As they arrived, they noticed that the previous customer had been painted with two dogs sitting in a basket on her pelvic region down to her navel. Each breast contained a dog's head, with the center of each breast being a dog's nose.

"I always used to like a little puppy nose," Doc remarked.

"When did you stop liking it?" Marilyn teased.

The couple exited the golf cart. Doc rolled his wheelchair toward the opened garage door where his neighbor, Randy, was creating his bodypainting masterpieces.

"It's Wonder Woman!" Randy exclaimed.

"Be careful. She has the golden lasso of truth in the golf cart," Doc responded.

"Indeed," Randy remarked.

"How long will this body painting last?" Marilyn inquired.

"Depending on the paint I use, I can make it wash off tonight or make it last for 3-5 days. It's up to you," Randy explained.

"What do you think, David?" Marilyn asked.

"If you have to leave campus sooner, I can give you some solvent that will take it off it a couple of minutes," Randy remarked.

"I like the idea of a three-day tryst with Wonder Woman," Doc replied.

Marilyn nodded affirmatively. Randy motioned for Marilyn to take off her shorts and tank top and lay on his spray table.

Randy was quite the artist. In less than fifteen minutes he had Marilyn dressed only in a painted outfit that looked identical to a Wonder Woman costume.

"I'm going to make it backless and paint your bottom to look similar to the front of the costume," Randy explained.

Marilyn gently crawled off the table and stood while Randy finished his work. He double checked for any inconsistencies and made a few adjusting sprays.

"What do you think?" Randy Anderson asked.

"How long before it dries completely?" Doc asked.

"I'd give it a good hour," Randy said.

"Will it rub off after that?" Doc inquired.

"Not really. It may fade from showering or activity, but it won't color the sheets or the furniture," he explained.

"We'll leave the golf cart and hit the walking trail for an hour," Doc said.

"No! I don't want anyone to see my costume before 6:00 pm," she exclaimed.

Doc sighed and told Randy, "We'll pick up the golf cart after the party."

"Not a problem," Randy said with a smile.

* * *

When they arrived back at their house, there was a petite, fully endowed thirty-something woman waiting on their porch for them. She was wearing a very tiny black and white French maid outfit, black stockings, and black high heels.

"The party's not till 6:00 pm," Marilyn remarked.

"No, NO, my name is Giselle. I provide maid service for several of your neighbors. I was the maid for your Uncle Donald," she explained.

"Come inside. We'll discuss your services," Doc replied.

Once inside, Giselle explained the services provided and the weekly rates. She had a regular weekly rate, but she offered a ten-percent discount for nude maid services.

"Why is the rate for a nude maid cheaper than one with clothes?" Doc queried.

"I don't like to wear clothes when I work," Giselle explained.

"You've sold me. I want the naked rate," Doc said.

When Giselle had left Marilyn said, "Naked rate, indeed."

"Always go for the best deal, Marilyn," Doc said with a nod.

"Ok, Mr. Dealmaker, get your costume on. We've got an hour," Marilyn instructed.

As Doc rolled toward the master bedroom, Marilyn followed him. While undressing, Doc noticed that she was watching him.

"What are you doing?" Doc asked.

"I'm watching you," Marilyn retorted.

"Why?" Doc inquired.

"You got to watch me put my costume on," Marilyn said.

"Oh please," Doc said with a slight sigh.

* * *

Promptly at 6:00 pm Marilyn and Doc made their way down the street to Bruno Eberhardt's house in the nearby cul-de-sac. The costumed crowd was already gathering. Ian Bradley, the regular Caliente DJ, was playing some tunes for the revelers.

Doc knew some of the neighbors but was not acquainted with all of them. It was the same with Marilyn. She knew more of her female neighbors and less of her male neighbors.

As they neared Bruno Eberhardt's abode, they saw a familiar face. It was their friend, Dave McDonald. He waved and smiled.

"What are you?" Doc answered.

"Before this night is over, I hope to be a sexually satisfied drunk," Dave replied.

"Oh my," Marilyn said under her breath.

A long-haired brunette in a very short witch's costume said to Doc, "I'm a witch."

Doc inquired, "Are you a good witch or a bad witch?"

"Oh, I'm very, very good," the witch replied.

Taking a second look, Doc remarked, "No doubt."

After the good witch smiled and walked away, Dave remarked, "That's one of my old girlfriends. I can vouch that she is very, very good."

Noticing Marilyn in the crowd, Bruno Eberhard made his way toward them. He was wearing a red and black cowboy shirt, a black cowboy hat, black boots, and chaps.

"You want to save a horse and ride a cowboy?" Bruno asked Marilyn.

"I've got my own plane," Marilyn said pointing at her costume.

"Braggart!" Bruno said as he walked away.

At that point the three noticed Bruno's bare bottom and the back of his naughty parts. It was more surprising than the time he had exercised the option at the Tiki Bar.

"That man's hung like a horse," Dave remarked.

"He may be one of those cowboys from Brokeback Mountain," Doc suggested.

"It doesn't matter. It still deserves its own zip code," Marilyn remarked.

A small framed blonde approached the trio with a large tray of brownies. She held out the tray in an effort to offer them some brownies.

"I'm Suzy Homemaker. Would you like to try my brownies?" she asked.

"No, they would not!" Dave exclaimed.

Suzy Homemaker frowned and moved along. Doc stared at Dave as if to challenge his rudeness.

"Doc, if Marilyn had eaten any of those brownies, she would think she was riding in her invisible plane," Dave remarked.

"I guess Betty Crocker doesn't have anything on her," Doc replied.

It wasn't long before Doc was approached by a woman dressed in a naughty schoolgirl outfit. Her plaid skirt was very short and it barely covered half of her buns.

"I've been naughty. Do you want to spank me?" she asked.

"Maybe later," Doc replied.

Marilyn noticed Charlotte in the crowd and waved to her. Charlotte approached them smiling.

"Doc, that's our cue to make our get away," Dave suggested.

"I agree. We'll be caught in the middle of girl talk for an hour," Doc responded.

"What's new today?" Charlotte asked.

"We hired Uncle Donald's French maid, Giselle," Marilyn reported.

"Giselle! Giselle, my ass. She's not from France. She's from Macon, Georgia," Charlotte remarked.

"We got a discount for letting her work in the nude," Marilyn said.

"You'll get more work out of her that way," Charlotte said with a chuckle.

As Doc and Dave walked around the cul-de-sac, Dave would stop and occasionally introduce him to a few neighbors. As they reached the opening of the cul-de-sac, Dave motioned for Doc to stop for him to take a breath and get another can of Pabst Blue Ribbon beer.

A lady approached Doc and asked, "Do you mind if I sit in your lap for a while?"

"That seat isn't taken," Doc said with a smile.

"As the woman sat in Doc's lap, she said, "I'm Tracy. I have heard you sing a couple of times, but we haven't actually met."

"I'm Dr. David Michaels but most people just say Doc," he explained.

"I can tell that you're glad to see me," Tracy said.

Not realizing that Tracy was sitting on the air pistol in the holster, he said, "I'm happy when beautiful women sit in my lap."

It wasn't long before Tracy began gently rubbing herself against the bulging pistol. The conversation lagged as she began to obviously enjoy the activity. Doc decided not to break her concentration after concluding that it wouldn't be long before she had finished the needful.

Dave walked back with the PBR in his hand. He wasn't really sure what was going on, but it was obvious that Tracy was enjoying the activity.

About that moment Tracy gently moans and falls limp in Doc's lap. It takes about thirty seconds for her to recover.

"You're naughty!" she exclaimed as she hopped out of Doc's lap and headed for the crowd. Suddenly, she turned, waved, and blew a kiss to Doc.

"I don't know what you were doing, Doc. But, it's pretty obvious you made a lasting impression," Dave McDonald remarked.

"I hope she doesn't give out recommendations," Doc said rolling his eyes.

"You better hope her boyfriend, Jeff Reiner, doesn't find out. As Lynyrd Skynyrd says in the song, "Gimme Three Steps", he's 'a man who cares,'" Dave said.

"She . . . I'm mean . . . it was . . . er, I mean . . . did all the work," Doc stammered.

"How's my little soldier?" Marilyn asked as she approached Doc and Dave.

"He's seen a little action tonight," Dave replied with Doc giving him an evil glance.

"I've got an application to become one of the Dickie Do girls," Marilyn said excitedly.

"Do either of you know anything about Dickie Do?" Dave asked.

"Uncle Donald always said he was a Dickie Do guy." Doc replied.

"Why was that?" she asked.

"He said, 'Because my belly sticks out further than my dickie do,'" Doc said with a laugh.

"No doubt," Marilyn replied.

"A Dickie Do girl is basically a call girl that is available to members of Dickie Do," Dave said.

"Well, that was a short-lived career," Doc remarked as he watched Marilyn put the application in a nearby trash can.

Bruno Eberhardt stood on a small ladder and began blowing a rather shrill whistle signaling it was 9:00 pm. Everyone stopped what they were doing and turned in Bruno's direction.

"What's he doing?" Marilyn asked.

"He's signaling that it's 9:00 pm," Dave replied.

"Why is that significant?" Doc asked.

"The rule is: When the whistle blows, everything goes," Dave explained.

"Marilyn's in trouble. Her costume is spray painted," Doc observed.

"You're the one in trouble, David," she responded.

"Why do you think that?" Doc asked.

"Looks like your little soldier is coming out to greet the neighbors," Marilyn said.

"He's been practicing standing at attention," Dave remarked.

"I should have gotten this camouflage painted on," Doc said with a large sigh.

13. Honkytonk Badonkadonk

Doc and Marilyn had settled in as the newest residents of the Caliente community. He was out for a solo brunch at Café Ole while Marilyn participated in a charity topless car wash for a few hours.

One of the weekend bartenders, Robert Wilson, had been injured in an auto accident the previous week. Although his principal injury consisted of a broken leg, it would be a few weeks before he would be behind the counter at the Caliente Tiki Bar.

Suzie, the Spa Manager, had talked Marilyn into helping with a charity car wash to help with Robert's lost wages during his absence.

Meanwhile, Doc opted to spend his morning having a delicious breakfast at the resort's white tablecloth restaurant. The restaurant had quite a few patrons but was not overly crowed.

As Doc sipped on his large glass of Florida orange juice, a thirty-something, attractive brunette approached his table and asked if she could talk with him. Doc nodded and the young lady seated herself.

"Aren't you the karaoke guy they call Doc?" she asked.

"That would be me. I sang one song a few weeks ago and now I'm the karaoke guy," he replied.

"My name is Lila Love. I do a lot of things at Caliente. A couple of those are teaching a twerking and pole dancing class for about four weeks five or six times a year," Lila explained.

"I understand pole dancing but what in the hell is twerking?" Doc queried.

"Twerking is a dance move where female dancers throw or thrust their hips back and shake their bottoms. It is quite the crowd pleaser," Lila Love replied.

"How does that involve me?" Doc asked politely.

"I want to announce the beginning of another four-week class session at Tiki Bar karaoke this afternoon. I need you to sing Trace Akins' song 'Honkytonk Badonkadonk,'" she replied.

"I know the song and I can sing it. But, it's karaoke, not a concert," Doc said with a chuckle.

"If I do as well with my struttin' and twerkin' as I hope, you'll be better than Trace Adkins himself," Miss Love promised.

"I'll be there at 5:00 pm but the crowd reaches its peak around 7:00 pm. I recommend that your twerking begin at that time," Doc suggested.

"That's great! After our performance is finished, I have a couple of other things to talk to you about," Lila said as she stood and made her exit.

* * *

After the first hour the charity car wash had made $160 in washes and donations. It wasn't as much as they had hoped but there was still two hours before it would shut down.

The event was in a very visible location near the tennis and pickle ball courts. Every vehicle that entered or left the resort would pass the car wash.

A gentleman in a red Porsche Boxster parked and motioned for Marilyn. She walked to the car and smiled pleasantly.

"I wanted to get a good look and negotiate a car wash," the middle-aged gentleman remarked.

"The car wash is $10 but most people add a small gratuity or donation to that amount," Marilyn said.

"How much for a nude car wash?" the man asked.

"Let me get the coordinator over here to answer that question. Her name is Suzie. I'll be right back," Marilyn offered.

The man nodded and smiled. He stared as Marilyn walked away in her ragged Daisy Duke style denim shorts.

"Marilyn explained that you want to purchase a totally nude car wash," Suzie said.

"I don't want to see anything including shoes," the gentleman explained.

"Which girl do you have in mind?" she inquired.

"Her," he replied, pointing to Marilyn.

"It'll be $100 cash for a stripped-down car wash by Marilyn," she offered.

Marilyn was quite surprised as she had only been topless at Caliente. She thought that the bending, stretching, and reaching might be bad naked rather than good naked. Nevertheless, she nodded her head affirmatively.

"What if I add getting foamy suds all over her body?" he asked.

Without hesitation, Suzie said, "Another $100."

"I'm in. Here's my $200. But, how much more if I get to watch her wash the soap off with that hose?" he inquired.

"It's $50 more if you watch and $100 if you use the hose," Suzie replied.

"Here's another $100. Let's get started," the gentleman exclaimed.

* * *

Doc made his way to a palapa near the Tiki Bar and began to sort through his email. At about 12:30 pm Marilyn appeared and joined Doc.

"How did the car wash go?" Doc asked.

"We made almost $700 today," Marilyn said with excitement.

"That's nice," Doc said as he scrolled through his list of emails.

"A middle-aged man gave $200 to see me totally naked!" Marilyn said.

"Did he ask for a refund?" Doc inquired.

"Actually he gave an extra $100 donation and even used the hose to wash away the suds on me," she replied in a slightly indignant manner.

Just as Marilyn finished speaking, Lila Love walked toward the palapa. Marilyn smiled and Doc nodded as she approached them.

"Marilyn, this is Lila Love. She teaches twerking and pole dancing classes here at Caliente. Her classes begin next week. She's performing a dance routine while I sing that Trace Adkins song, Honkytonk Badonkadonk," Doc explained.

"That's nice," Marilyn said to Doc slightly rolling her eyes.

"I'm really excited," Lila said.

"What are you wearing during the performance?" Marilyn asked.

"Just a small white G-string," Lila replied.

"That'll make alcohol sales go up today," Doc suggested.

"Indeed," Marilyn remarked.

"We've got about two hours before Lila wants us to perform. Let's go to Lust and look at slutwear," Doc suggested.

"Charlotte prefers that you call it sexy wear or resort wear," Marilyn retorted.

"Like Gertrude Stein said, 'A rose is a rose is a rose,'" Doc said philosophically.

The couple entered Lust boutique and there were several customers browsing the shop's merchandise.

163

Sunday afternoons were always good times for finding treasures at Lust.

"Doc, are you casting caution to the wind and setting free your lust today?" Charlotte asked in a loud voice.

"Don't worry, it's not conquered yet," Doc replied in an equally loud voice.

A very attractive forty-something blonde was looking and feeling of a very fancy, sequined, red bra and panty set. Doc made the mistake of making eye contact with her.

"Can you help me with this?" the lady asked as she put the cups around her large, firm breasts.

"What do you need me to do?" Doc asked.

"Hook me, please," the hot blonde implored.

Doc retrieved his reading glasses, placed them on, and began to fumble with getting the four hooks fastened. It was apparent that he was struggling.

"I hope he's better at taking one off than putting one on," Charlotte remarked.

After finishing the task, the woman looked at herself in one of the side mirrors. Doc checked out the finished product, too.

"It's in the next to last position. It can be loosened," Doc explained.

"Help me get it off. I'm buying this outfit and wearing it to the next party," she explained.

With the flick of his hand, the fancy bra hit the floor. It appeared effortless.

Before anyone could say anything, Doc remarked, "That's my specialty."

"Charlotte, do you have any sexy wear for men?" Marilyn inquired.

"We only have what's on that rounder in the back-left corner. But, Androgynous down the street has a lot of that type of fashion for men," she instructed.

"We'll give it a try after your performance," Marilyn promised.

"Sounds like you're getting lucky, Doc," Charlotte said.

"Come on, lucky man. We've actually got time to do a little shopping at Androgynous before you sing," Marilyn opined.

* * *

Androgynous Boutique was only a couple of miles from the main gate at Caliente Resort. It was at the end of a very small strip mall but took two complete store units.

Doc said later that he felt like a Ken doll in the hands of a stripper with Marilyn looking for outfits for him. Most of her selections ended up in the "No" or "Hell No" piles.

Nevertheless Doc was attracted to one particular outfit. It was silver lamé, a fabric woven with ribbons of metallic fabric. The outfit included shorts, a matching bowtie, and matching cuffs that snapped on both wrists.

"Where's the shirt?" Doc asked.

"It's for a teddy bear look," the male clerk said.

"What's a teddy bear look?" Doc inquired.

"It's for a muscular man with a little fur on his chest," the clerk said with a giggle.

"Women like a little grass on the playground occasionally," Marilyn remarked.

"Men, too!" the salesclerk opined.

"Oh, hell," Doc said with a sigh.

"We'll take it. You can wear it to the comedy show after karaoke tonight," Marilyn remarked.

* * *

Marilyn and Doc arrived the Tiki Bar about ten minutes before Lila and Doc's performance. With a minute or so, Lila Love showed up in her tiny white G-string and gave Doc a big hug and a kiss.

"I'll tell KJ Nick to get us in the rotation," she said as she walked away.

"Friendly little thing," Marilyn said with an eye roll.

"I suppose," Doc said in a monotone reply.

KJ Nick Colorado pointed toward Doc indicating that he would be the next performer. The Tiki Bar was full, and had an overflow spilling out both the front and back doors. The covered patio area behind the Tiki Bar was almost full. The heated winter pool nearby was almost full, too.

KJ Nick handed Doc the expensive microphone and said, "You know the rule."

"Drop this and I'm a dead man," Doc said with a chuckle.

As the music started, Doc mimicked Trace's intro by saying, "Turn it up, son."

Lila Love put her drink on the bar and walked quite seductively toward the small stage at the rear of the Tiki Bar. All eyes were upon her as she gave an exaggerated hip and arm swing.

Doc continued, "Here she comes now, here she comes."

The clapping, whistling, and yelling covered Doc's rendition of the first verse. As he neared the chorus, KJ Nick ran the sound up very loudly to overcome the crowd noise.

Doc hit the chorus and Lila Love alternately thrust here hips and flexed and wiggled her nearly bare bottom to the lyrics. It truly was a sight to behold. Doc crooned:

"Honkytonk badonkadonk
Keeping perfect rhythm makes you wanna swing
along
Got it goin' on like Donkey Kong
And ooohwee shut my mouth, slap your grandma
There ought to be a law, get the sheriff on the
phone
Lord have mercy how'd she even get them britches
on
With that honkytonk badonkadonk!"

Doc decided to ad lib a bit during the musical break: "Aw son! That's what I'm talking about right there. That's why I sing karaoke. It's not for the recognition. It's not for the free drinks. It's for that badonkadonk!"

Needless to say, between Lila Love's fantastic gyrations and Doc's rendition of the Trace Adkins favorite, it was another performance to be remembered.

As the song finished, KJ Nick announced, "That's Doc Michaels and Lila Love doing Honkytonk Badonkadonk! If you want to learn to move like that ladies, Lila's dance pole and twerking classes start at 6:00 pm Wednesday night and last for four weeks."

Moving through the crowd and receiving back pats and high fives, Doc, Marilyn, and Lila retired to the covered patio outside the Tiki Bar.

"To put it bluntly, I'm a porn star," Lila Love said.

"Is that a gratifying line of work for you?" Marilyn asked.

"Actually, I went to the New York Film Academy to be a film director. But over the past few years that never panned out," Lila replied.

"Why hasn't that career taken off?" Doc asked.

"There's a lot of directors vying for a limited number of opportunities. I'm not connected to the industry and I haven't done any films to get me noticed," she explained.

"How's your porn business doing?" Doc inquired.

"I have my own site. I shoot videos with my husband. He graduated NYFA in acting. We're monogamous. Also, I do some directing for other porn companies," Lila said.

"What was your arrangement with Uncle Donald?" Marilyn asked.

"He was going to let us shoot a video in his home. I had been contacted about directing a shoot for a nationwide distributor," she replied.

"So you want us to let you shoot the video at our home?" Doc inquired.

"Actually, I wanted to do something different," she said.

"What exactly would that be?" Marilyn asked.

"I want to shoot a XXX wheelchair fetish porn movie and a PG-13 movie about you two," she said with a serious note.

"Are you expecting us to appear in the porn movie?" Marilyn asked.

"No, I have professional actors for the porn video. You can be a paid creative consultant fee on that one. It has a pretty good budget for a porn flick," Lila said.

"Let's get to the Doc and Marilyn part," Doc instructed.

"We can use you as talent or as consultants to the story line," Lila offered.

"Do you think anyone would be interested in that PG-13 video?" Marilyn asked.

"Actually, I want to pitch it as a pilot for a single camera adult comedy on one of the streaming services. I have the credentials. I just need the subject. Nobody has done a comedy with the lead character in a wheelchair," she remarked.

"How many are in your crew?" Doc asked.

"Just me, the camera guy, a lighting guy, an oiler, a fluffer, and a few actors/actresses," she replied.

"What is a fluffer and an oiler?" Marilyn inquired.

"A fluffer keeps the male porn actor erect between cuts. An oiler is like a makeup person that applies lotion or oil on an actress to give her a three-dimensional appearance in a two dimensional medium," Lila said without hesitation.

"Marilyn wants to be a fluffer," Doc said.

"I certainly have plenty of practice with you," she remarked rather sternly.

Ignoring the banter, Lila asked, "What do you think?"

"We don't have a problem with you using the house. We're not particularly fans of porn flicks but that's a personal decision. We'll write it off as keeping one of Uncle Donald's promises," Doc replied.

"What are your thoughts on the comedy pilot?" she asked.

"I like the idea. I think it will be well received. I think you should find talented actors and actresses," Marilyn opined.

"I agree. But we'd be willing to help with the story line and some ideas," Doc added.

"Give me about two months to get everything set. I'll stay in touch," Lila promised.

14. Comedy Club

Since Caliente is mostly a mid-week to weekend resort, Mondays and Tuesdays are usually slow until the evenings. Mondays provide a weekly eight ball pool tournament and Tuesdays evenings are a prize-filled Trivia Contest.

Unlike most Tuesdays, this one was different. The resort had scheduled an evening meal in the nightclub to be followed by a comedian-laden comedy show for the members and guests.

Doc and Marilyn had planned to attend the show for almost two weeks. In fact, part of the reason for purchasing Doc the silver lamé outfit with shorts, bowtie, and cuffs was for him to wear it at the comedy show.

Although Marilyn really liked the outfit, Doc held a somewhat lackluster attitude about it. He referred to it as making him into "Long Dong Silver" as he had to make sure his junk stayed inside the shorts as he sat in his wheelchair.

It was mid-afternoon when someone knocked on their door. The visitor was greeted by Doc and welcomed into the foyer.

"I'm Julian Joeb. I am a photographer," the young man said introducing himself.

"I am Dr. David Michaels, and this is my wife, Marilyn. We are pleased to make your acquaintance," Doc said pointing to the large living room sofa for Julian to be seated.

"I'm here on business," Julian said.

"What kind of business?" Marilyn asked.

"Actually I want to discuss using you as a model," he replied.

"Me? A model?!" Marilyn responded with a small laugh.

"What do you have in mind?" Doc queried.

"I have two propositions. First, I want to use her images on social media for the resort. Secondly, I would like to include some grayscale images of her in erotic photographs that are framed and sold in my gallery," Julian explained.

"Will these be nude images?" Marilyn asked.

"The photos for Caliente will be sexy but not nude. A lot of social media, particularly in the United States, still prohibits nude photographs. Some tolerate side boob or topless but not many," Julian replied.

"Is there any compensation for modeling for the resort?" she inquired.

"There is compensation of a sort. You'll get a few hundred dollars food and beverage credit on your Caliente house account," Julian explained.

"How much time is involved?" Doc asked.

"Two or three half days a year," Julian estimated.

"I'll do it!" Marilyn said excitedly.

"What about the erotic gallery photography?" Doc asked.

"We'll have a one- or two-day photo shoot. I will crop the photos. They may be committed to canvas or printed and framed for sale in the gallery," he replied.

"What is the compensation?" Marilyn asked.

"I pay the model one third of the sale price of the artwork," Julian explained.

"What is the typical pricing?" Doc asked.

"From about $250 to $1500 with an average price of $500 per sale," he responded.

"How nude is nude?" Marilyn inquired.

"These photos minimize the facial aspect. It is usually about contours, shapes, and unusual poses. The images are pieces of fine art, not pornography," Julian said indignantly.

"I will pose for your gallery. Fortunately, we don't need the money, so I want my share donated to Breast Cancer Awareness," Marilyn explained.

"Excellent! I will leave these releases with you for you to complete. Drop them at the front desk. We'll work out a schedule next week," Julian instructed.

"Can I get one full length nude pinup style image on canvas out of this deal?" Doc asked.

"That will be around $1000," Julian suggested.

"Is that before or after her discount?" Doc asked.

"There is no discount. Marilyn's percentage goes to Breast Cancer Awareness. We're saving the Ta-Tas," Julian replied with a large smile as he exited the front door.

* * *

As the dinner hour approached, Doc and Marilyn dressed in their finery and made their way to Club Fiesta for the dinner comedy show. Doc donned his Long Dong Silver outfit, so called, and waited on Marilyn to finish.

Marilyn opted for a patriotic look. She wore a long white tank top that stopped at the waist and turned into a full 360 degrees of fringe that ended at her upper thighs. Underneath the fringe was a red thong. Her shoes were red, platform high heels that Doc called hooker heels.

She wore matching garnet jewelry that included a necklace, bracelet, and ring. When she walked, the fringe moved and put some motion into her stride.

Doc called Gilbert to pick them up in the six-passenger golf cart for the trip to the clubhouse. It was about a ten-minute ride that Gilbert often turned into a fifteen- minute excursion.

"That outfit makes me want to sing 'God Bless America,'" Gilbert remarked upon watching Marilyn climb into the golf cart.

"Thank you, Gilbert," Marilyn replied.

Upon arriving at the clubhouse at promptly 7:30 pm, the doors at Club Fiesta had been opened and Chadwick was seating the dinner patrons.

"Do you have a reservation?" Chadwick asked of Doc.

"Of course I have a reservation! I made it with you," Doc responded.

"Nice outfit. I love that teddy bear look," Chadwick said.

"Thank you, Chadwick," Marilyn said as Doc rolled his eyes and entered the club to be seated.

Doc had made his reservation once he became aware of the comedy dinner show. Their table was on the ·dance floor very close to the stage.

After only a minute or two, their favorite waitress, Kelly Jeong, appeared to take their drink orders. She was holding back a giggle and Doc would not make eye contact.

"You seem very happy tonight, Kelly," Marilyn noted.

Hearing that comment, Kelly broke into an almost uncontrollable laugh. It was obvious that she was very amused at Doc's silver outfit.

After regaining control, Kelly mustered the fortitude to speak, "Doc, that outfit just makes me want to pinch those pink nipples."

"Indeed," Doc replied.

"I'll have a club soda and David will have a ginger ale," Marilyn said.

An unknown woman approached their table and remarked, "Honey, that outfit just makes me want to grab you and rub all over you."

"That's the effect I was hoping for," Doc said slightly sarcastically.

"That's the second nice compliment he's had tonight," Marilyn said with a smile.

"It won't be his last," the lady said as she winked at Marilyn and made her way back to her table.

Their good friend, Mako, approached their table bearing a drink. It was obviously a glass of ginger ale.

"That's not Pabst Blue Ribbon," Doc remarked.

"It's ginger ale and it's for you," Mako replied.

"What's the occasion for you buying me a drink?" Doc asked.

"It's not from me. It's that big brunette over there," Mako said.

Doc looked in the direction that Mako nodded. There was very attractive lady giving Doc a discreet wave. Doc returned the wave.

"Tell Xena, the warrior princess, thank you for the drink," Doc said giving Mako an icy stare.

"I think she likes you, Doc," Mako said with a chuckle.

"No doubt," Marilyn remarked.

Kelly arrived with Marilyn's club soda and Doc's ginger ale. She had a confused look on her face. Mako pointed to the nearby table.

"Doc, women are buying you drinks and it's still early," Kelly remarked.

"It's that teddy bear chest," Mako interjected.

Doc grabbed his cloth napkin and started popping it at Mako. After a couple of pops on his arm and chest, Mako retreated quickly.

"That's rude," Marilyn remarked.

"He's a busybody," Doc replied.

"Have you decided on a selection?" Kelly asked.

"What do you have?" Marilyn asked.

"It's a dinner show with limited selections. We have steak, chicken, and salmon," Kelly replied.

"I'll have salmon," Marilyn said.

"I'll have salmon. Maybe the Omega 3 oil will help my memory," Doc responded.

"Are you experiencing memory loss, Doc?" Kelly asked.

"No, I just want to make sure that I remember not to go 'teddy bear' again," he explained.

Near the end of the meal, Chadwick approached the table with a very somber look. It was obvious that something had gone very wrong.

"Doc, I've got a problem and I don't know where to turn," Chadwick said.

"If it wears a skirt or has wheels, it's gonna be a problem," Doc replied.

"How can we help you, Chadwick?" Marilyn asked in a consoling tone.

"Our first comedian for the evening didn't realize that this was a clothing optional resort. He cancelled his performance," Chadwick explained.

"What about your other comedian?" Doc asked.

"His wife went into labor and is having a baby as we speak. He cancelled his performance, too," he replied.

"Other than losing the part of the tickets devoted to the comedy show, how does that affect us?" Doc queried.

"You're always the life of the party. Can't you do some comedy? Can't you sing a few songs?" Chadwick asked.

"Other than this Long Dong Silver outfit, I can't imagine that I could pull off a comedy routine. I'm not your guy, Chadwick," Doc explained.

"Just get up and talk about your family. Talk about the funny stories about being in a wheelchair. Sing a couple of your dirty songs," Marilyn implored.

"I'll get heckled and booed off the stage!" Doc exclaimed.

"If you can go a half hour, DJ Ian is on the way to play dance music to fill out the show. We can get by with a lot less complaints," Chadwick explained.

"Damn! This is outrageous," Doc exclaimed.

"Announce what happened and that he's filling in at Caliente's request. I'll get Mako and Dave to get him on the stage," Marilyn promised.

As Chadwick took the stage to make the announcement, Mako Jenkins placed Doc's wheelchair at the top of the four stairs. Dave McDonald helped Doc navigate the railed stairs and take a seat in the chair.

While Doc rolled his wheelchair to the center of the stage, the crowd clapped, cheered, whistled, and otherwise encouraged him. Doc hoped that they'd be gentle. This definitely wasn't karaoke.

"The real truth is that the other comedians heard that you were a tough crowd and bailed," Doc said as the crowd cheered and clapped.

"I'm not as much of a comedian as I am a storyteller. I decided to tell you a little about my brother tonight," Doc said.

"My brother is addicted to dating mean and crazy girls. Just when you think he'll never be able to find one any crazier, he'll bring in another one and surprise you. He dated one that was so crazy that our mother nicknamed her 'Old Crazy!'" Doc explained as the crowd laughed and clapped.

"I love my brother but he's difficult, self-centered and downright irritating. But despite all that, he finally found one that was only moderately crazy, and they got married. In an effort to improve his attitude, his wife of a couple years threatened that if he didn't straighten up, he'd be cut-off," Doc said amidst the laughter.

"Any of you ever been cut off? If you've ever been cut off, raise your hand" Doc said.

There were a few hands that went in the air amidst the clapping and loud laughter.

"This room is full of liars. There's a couple of guys up front that are cut-off tonight," Doc said pointing randomly into the crowd.

The clapping and laughter increased, and one heckler yelled, "Have you ever been cut-off?"

"If I blow this show, I'll definitely be cut-off tonight," Doc replied.

The crowd really broke into loud laughter, clapping, and cheering at that response. Doc thought so far so good.

Returning to his story line, Doc continued, "When my sister in law threatened my brother with being cut off for his bad attitude, he said, "You'll have to find out where I'm getting it first!"

Now the punch line garnered Doc a standing ovation and a riotous response. Even Marilyn laughed and clapped after hearing the story a dozen times over the years.

"I've never dated crazies. They just turned that way after I married them . . . OK, that just got ME cut-off," Doc explained.

Needless to say, Doc had the crowd entertained and happy when he was on stage. Doc worried that he'd not be able to keep up the pace for another fifteen minutes.

"I dated a lot of women in college and afterwards. Marilyn said that I was a man-whore. That's not true. I'm like Dave McDonald. We've both been turned down more often than the sheets at a Holiday Inn," Doc continued.

The audience clapped and cheered. Dave stood and took a bow."

"You may think it's a drag being in a wheelchair, but it's not . . . Do you know the best pickup line if you're in a wheelchair? You ask a woman if she's ever had sex with a guy in a wheelchair. Before she can respond, you ask, 'Do you want to?'" Doc explained and continued to speak above laughter and clapping.

Let me share some little-known benefits of being in a wheelchair:

1. You can have a conversation with a woman and see her titties and face at the same time. She doesn't catch you moving your eyes or adjusting your head.

2. It puts you at touch level. Women have a hard time resisting putting their hands on your shoulders, fixing your collar, or touching your hair. One caveat: Always wear something soft. Get rid of those starched dress shirts!

3. They'll jump at the opportunity to sit in your lap for a slow dance. Hell, if their feet get too tired, they sit in your lap for a fast dance.

4. You are always a good candidate for mercy sex! I know. None of you have ever had to resort to mercy sex.

"When I was younger, I liked the idea of doing the wild thing with a fat girl. Finally, I met this really attractive brunette nurse that was slightly on the husky side. Well, Texas ain't all that big – at least when you compare it to Alaska," Doc explained.

"During dinner she remarked that she was accessible. I didn't know if she meant her or her apartment, Doc said.

The crowd had been with Doc for the last twenty-five minutes and he was still providing quality entertainment. He needed another five minutes and a strong ending to hit the proverbial home run.

"When we got to her apartment, she excused herself and went into the bathroom. In a minute or so she opened the door. She was completely naked and was holding a syringe in her right hand," Doc explained.

He continued, "She said, 'It's penicillin. It's just a precaution. I knew you would understand.'"

"I turned this wheelchair on two wheels, threw open the apartment door, and laid rubber all the way across the parking lot. I folded this chair, threw it across the bench seat, fired that mother up, and took off like a bat outta hell! I am cured of wanting to ever date a nurse," Doc concluded.

Doc completed his first comic monologue in fine fashion. The crowd was on its feet clapping, cheering, and whistling.

Chadwick took the stage and said, "Let's hear it for Doc!"

Once again, the crowd showed their appreciation for Doc's monologue. Doc thought to himself that he'd never again wear the Long Dong Silver outfit or fill in for professional comedians again.

DJ Ian arrived for the last ten minutes of Doc's routine. As Mako and Dave helped Doc down the stairs and into his wheelchair, Ian started playing Unchained Melody by the Righteous Brothers.

Marilyn met Doc on the dance floor and leaped into his lap. He was quite surprised given some of his remarks.

"I thought I was cut-off," Doc said.

"Baby, you are cut-in tonight! I'm taking this seat before someone else tries. We'll stay for a few songs and round up Gilbert," Marilyn replied.

15. Hurricane Party (Part I)

After a few months at Caliente Resort, guests would often ask Doc what he thought about the resort. He never hesitated with his response. He would always say, "If you aren't happy at this place, you won't be happy anywhere."

There was ample evidence to support Doc's conclusion. Tampa has a humid subtropical climate. There is sunshine 300 days a year. Caliente's year consists of three seasons: Summer, January, and February. Even the first two months of the year see average highs in the lower 70s and average lows in the lower 50s.

In addition to its clothing optional friendly weather, Caliente has the reputation of being the fun capital of south Florida. There are always several events or activities each week. At the resort and within the community, it is always, "Party On!"

Notwithstanding Doc's opinion, supported by ample evidence, there is one lurking enemy that stalks Tampa Bay from June through November. It rarely appears but has the power, not only to disrupt the fun, but to destroy lives and property. It is a hurricane.

The last major hurricane to attack the Tampa area was in 1921. It was before the National Weather Service named hurricanes and it is remembered as the Tampa Bay Hurricane of 1921.

It came ashore as a Category 4 storm with wind gusts of 111 to 129 mph and sustained winds of 75 mph in downtown Tampa. The storm surge was ten to 12 feet. Most of Tampa was flooded, businesses were ruined, and hundreds of homes were destroyed.

Tampa has had a few near misses and several tropical storms in the following 100 years. But when a watch is issued, local residents and businesses take note.

At Caliente any prediction of an approaching storm at Category 3 or below gives rise to a Hurricane Party. The resort lies well outside the mandatory evacuation zone so it's simply hunker down and wait.

The indoor social event usually lasts 24-36 hours and gives rise to food, drink, and fun activities customized for Caliente residents, members and guests.

Doc watched the Weather Channel for routine updates regarding Hurricane Dani's approach. Marilyn packed a couple of duffle bags for the short trip to the Caliente Clubhouse for the Hurricane Party that was set to begin at 5:00 pm.

Hurricane Dani was set to strike within a 50-mile radius of downtown Tampa. The outer band wind was predicted to be at 20 mph by 7:00 pm with the storm expected to make landfall between 2:00 am and 4:00 am.

"I'm packing the sleeping bags," Marilyn shouted from the master bedroom.

"I thought we were staying at the hotel?" Doc asked.

"It's full. But it'll be more fun staying at the main building," she replied.

There was a ring of the doorbell and a rapid knocking on the front door. It could only be one of two people: Dave McDonald or Mako Jenkins.

Doc opened the door. Mako and Dave yelled, "Surprise!"

"There's nothing like a hurricane to bring out the crazies," Doc opined.

"David, why are you always rude to your best friends?" Marilyn asked with a scolding tone.

"Because God made me so good at it," he replied.

"Come in, please. Don't pay any attention to the curmudgeon," Marilyn instructed.

"He's just worried about all those hot women that'll be at the Hurricane Party wanting to sit in his lap," Mako said.

"Yeah, I heard about how two were squirming around in his lap last month and burst his silicone seat cushion," Dave said.

"Tell me! Tell me! I didn't hear about that!" Mako exclaimed.

Before Dave could respond, Doc asked sarcastically, "Do you want to hear it from this horse's mouth or that horse's ass?"

"I want to hear it from you. It's almost always better to hear it from you than to have actually been there," Mako responded.

"Indeed," Marilyn said beneath her breath.

"We were at Club Fiesta on Ladies Night during the Memorial Day Weekend Celebration. DJ Ian thought it would be interesting to slow things down on the dance floor by playing Elvis singing Can't Help Falling In Love.

"An attractive middle-aged lady sat down in my lap for a slow dance. Almost immediately, a second beautiful lady, near the same age, scooted the first lady to the side and sat down, too," Doc explained.

"Were they hot? Did you fondle them?" Mako asked.

"That's exactly why no woman would ever set in your lap in a wheelchair," Doc replied.

"You could loan me you chair, and we could do some research," Mako offered.

"It wouldn't take a half hour of you being in this chair before you'd grope some woman and get kicked out of the clubhouse for thirty days," Doc said.

"Ignore him and continue with you story, Doc," Dave McDonald suggested.

"The two ladies seated in my lap were doing fine. They were even giving me hugs and pecks on the cheeks," Doc explained.

"I didn't know that," Marilyn remarked.

"You were listening to nautical tales from your boat captain friend," Doc retorted.

"Were the tales hot and sexy? Did they really turn you on?" Mako asked in rapid succession.

"Mako, if you don't hush, I'm going to gag you!" Dave said sternly.

"Before the song ended, a young, very petite, four-foot, nine-inch, ninety-pound, Canadian blonde decided she could fit in the middle," Doc said before again being interrupted.

"That's when it happened. That's when that cushion squirted and slimed your chair. I just know it! That's when it happened!" Mako said excitedly.

"The silicone cushion ruptured, silicone jell covered the inside back of the wheelchair and my ass, and one of the older women yelled, 'We made him squirt! We made Doc squirt!'" he reported.

At that point Mako was laughing uncontrollably and so was Dave. Doc showed little emotion.

When the laughter subsided, Doc said, "Marilyn, tell these two friends the rest of the story."

"I came over to see what had happened. Because I had been talking to James, I suppose they thought I was Doc's sister or daughter. One of the women handed me a note and said, "Here's my cell phone number. That other lady is my sister. Have him call us. We'd like to buy him breakfast tomorrow morning."

I said, "That's really nice. I will tell him."

"She said, 'He'll need a little nourishment after a night with us'," Marilyn reported.

"Oh this thing just gets better and better! Did you give them a night to remember, Doc?" Mako queried.

"When they walked away, Marilyn said, 'David, I don't mind you enjoying yourself, but I'm not going to be a secretary for your bitches,' Doc replied.

Needless to say, the two men were back in belly laugh mode with Doc beginning to get slightly irritated. Marilyn even giggled, too.

When the laughter again subsided, Doc said, "It took about two hours to get that silicone off the wheelchair and my ass. I ordered and new dense foam cushion that is guaranteed to be bitch proof!"

"I'll be telling this story at the Hurricane Party," Mako promised.

"Now that we've got that out of the way, why are you two here anyway?" Doc asked.

"We're here to relocate your ham radio station and outdoor weather station to the clubhouse," Dave explained.

"Who wants that done?" Marilyn asked.

"It's directly from Steve Riley. He said he's not taking any chances on Hurricane Dani," Mako said.

"It'll take about 30 minutes to disconnect everything and then set up a portable station in the main building," Doc said.

"What do we need to do?" Dave asked.

"You need to hold the step ladder while Mako removes the Weather Station from the edge of the house. We'll take the ICOM 7700, the chrome lollipop microphone, the chrome CW key, and the large rectangular color monitor. I will disconnect everything while you handle the weather station," Doc instructed.

The job went faster than expected and within 15 minutes they were ready to load equipment. Dave had already secured the weather station in the back seat of his Ford Explorer.

"Dave, I want you to take the ICOM 7700 and Mako can take the rest with him," Doc instructed.

"I wanted to take the radio. I wanted to turn that big knob," Mako whined.

"You have the innate ability to destroy a steel door. You are not playing with a $6000 piece of equipment," Doc said bluntly.

"Can I play with that knob sometime tonight?" Mako asked.

"The only knob you're authorized to play with is that one that peeks out past those four rings," Doc replied.

* * *

The last thing to do after the radio equipment had been relocated and positioned was to connect the coaxial feed line to the Horizon 8006 vertical antenna. Although the amateur radio Hurricane net was only monitoring the 20 meter and 80-meter bands, the Horizon antenna made all ham bands from 2 meters through 80 meters available.

"What else can we do?" Steve Riley asked.

"We need to make sure the antenna is secured to the outside railing, and duct tape that 50-foot feed line around the baseboard so no one will catch a fall," Doc responded.

Steve Riley motioned for two security guards to perform the tasks mentioned by Doc. The two black uniformed guards nodded and proceeded to follow the instructions.

"Is there anything else you can think of?" Steve inquired.

"If Mako Jenkins comes near this equipment, have him arrested and executed," Doc instructed.

"Understood," Steve replied.

"David, you are just mean and rude to Mako," Marilyn responded.

"Imagine how he'd be if I was kind and gentle," Doc replied.

"The man has a point, Marilyn," Dave McDonald remarked.

* * *

Mako arrived at 6:00 pm in his golf cart at 69 Sand Hill Crane Drive to take Doc, Marilyn, and their three duffle bags to the main building. Two of the bags weighed about 30 pounds each but the third duffle bag was pushing 70 pounds.

"Are the family jewels in this bag?" Mako asked as he struggled to load the bag into the cart.

Doc pointed to his crotch and said, "The family jewels are here and safely away from you."

"I resent you suggesting that I prefer men over women," Mako said.

"I am suggesting that you are not trustworthy to get near my valuables," Doc said.

"You won't even let me twist that big knob tonight. Steve Riley told me what you said," Mako announced.

"I'll make a deal with you about that," Doc said.

"Will you? Will you really do that for me?" Mako inquired intently.

"I'll let you hold the microphone and squeeze it when I need to talk," Doc said.

"Oh that's great! I can do that without any problem," Mako said.

"He's probably had a lot of experience squeezing things," Marilyn said with a giggle.

"No doubt," Doc said.

"Now you've got Marilyn picking on me. You're just mean to me," Mako responded.

"Are you expecting to key that microphone tonight or not?" Doc asked.

"You are one of the kindest, gentlest, and finest men I have ever met. You are truly a caring individual," Mako replied.

"Marilyn, remind me to have security bring a second chair to the station so Mako can sit beside me when necessary," Doc instructed.

"Do you need me to ask them for anything else?" Marilyn inquired.

"Check if they have an extra shock collar," Doc said with a chuckle.

Mako thought to himself, "That man is just plain mean. He's a tyrant . . . But I get to play with the radio tonight!"

As the three made their way to the clubhouse for the Hurricane Party, Mako broke the silence by asking, "What's really in that heavy duffel bag?"

"Slut wear, shoes, and jewelry," Doc replied.

"Marilyn, why do you need so much of that stuff?" Mako asked.

"The party could last a long time. It could be two days. I need to keep fresh and exciting," she responded.

"She is like that song by Kool & The Gang, "Fresh", that says,

'She's fresh, fresh, exciting. So inviting to me,'" Doc said.

"Me too," Mako responded.

"You are such as sweet man," Marilyn said.

"Please tell that to Doc regularly," Mako pleaded.

Doc ignored the comment as the golf cart stopped at the front entrance. The trio was met by Gilbert.

"It's supposed to start raining and the wind blowing within the hour," Gilbert said.

"We going to be QRV or on the air in about ten minutes," Doc responded.

"Steve has a large monitor and computer set up near that radio station. You can see the readings from the weather station and use the computer if you need it," Gilbert reported.

"Did Dave McDonald bring the two deep cycle marine batteries and a charger for emergency backup?" Doc asked as he moved from the cart to his wheelchair.

"Yes, and there's battery backup on the monitor and computer, too," he responded.

"Is there a place for us to sleep tonight?" Marilyn asked.

"Sleep? I thought with that third duffle bag of slut wear and accessories that you'd party all night," Doc opined.

"I was asking for you dear. It's been a long time since you were able to pull an all-nighter," Marilyn replied.

"We're putting you on the floor behind the small bar near the dance floor," he responded.

"That's great!" Marilyn remarked.

"What do I need to do about Mako? Should I cuff him now as a preventive measure or wait till he really gets in trouble?" Gilbert asked.

"I'll get a couple of the older women to keep an eye on him. If you happen to see one or two middle school teachers, send them in my direction," Doc instructed.

"See, Marilyn, he's turning the whole world against me," Mako whined.

Marilyn hugged Mako and quietly whispered in his ear, "Don't screw up."

DJ Ian had arrived at Club Fiesta and was playing music. Several couples were dancing. Others were in the booths or the tables and having food and drink.

The big screen monitor read as follows:

7:00 pm DJ Ian plays your favorite tunes.

8:00 pm Pole Dance Contest

9:00 pm Lust Fashion Show

10:00 pm Adult Pinata Break

10:30 pm Between The Legs Bowling

11:00 pm Show Your Coconuts & Shake Your
Booty

Midnight Onward: Activities Are Weather
Dependent TBA

Note: A two-minute silent break will be taken on the hour and half hour for weather reports.

"I'm so excited! I've never been to a Hurricane Party!" Marilyn exclaimed.

"I'll be excited if Hurricane Dani makes landfall anywhere within 100 miles of Tampa," Mako said.

"What will get you excited, David?" Marilyn asked.

"Knowing that I may end up having three free meals off Steve Riley for setting up a Hurricane Watch Station here," Doc said with a large smile.

"That's more fun than having sex in the rain," Mako remarked.

"No, it's not," Marilyn opined.

16. Hurricane Party (Part II)

"Mako, we are going on the air for the Hurricane net. Let's bring up the station," Doc said.

Doc rolled toward the storage room to the right of the large dance floor and behind the side bar in Club Fiesta. They closed to door to keep out the music and crowd noise and began bringing up the amateur radio station.

Doc turned on the transceiver, set the band switch to 80 meters, and chose LSB as the type of transmission for the event. Mako waited patiently to play a role in the station's operation.

"Mako, our purpose is to serve as a ground reporting station to help provide real time weather information such as wind speed, barometric pressure readings, and rainfall when requested. We are not broadcasting. We are not in control of the Hurricane Watch Net."

"I understand," Mako replied solemnly.

"See that big knob?" Doc asked.

Mako nodded affirmatively.

"Turn it until it reaches 3.815 MHz on that large display," Doc instructed.

Mako slowly turned the VFO as instructed and exclaimed, "I hear people talking!"

"That's net control, the operator in charge, taking check-ins and reports from stations like us," Doc explained.

"Are there any stations in or near the Tampa Bay area?" the man from National Hurricane Watch asked.

Mako gently squeezed the bar on the long handled silver lollipop style microphone as Doc said, "W4SRX portable, Tampa, Florida."

"W4SRX acknowledged. Report," the gentleman instructed.

"Wind speed 25 mph sustained with gusts to 35 mph, pressure 29.25, rain fall .20 inches. W4SRX," Doc reported.

"Next station in the Tampa area," he said.

Doc lowered the volume and looked at Mako. He was not smiling but had a stern look on his face.

"Did you soil yourself, Mako?" Doc asked with a chuckle.

"This is real. There's a hurricane coming. People are depending on us to get vital information out so the National Weather Service can track the path of the storm and warn the public," Mako said.

"That is why you can't just turn knobs, press buttons, and play with the station. You have to be licensed, trained, and prepared for these type things. But, most of the time it's still a fun hobby that permits communication with other hams worldwide," Doc said.

"What do we do next?" Mako asked.

"We watch the pole dance contest and keep an eye on those TV monitors around the club. If there are any significant changes, we'll be back in here with the information," Doc instructed.

When Doc and Mako left the makeshift radio room, Ian requested that participants for the pole dance contest line up near the stage. The ladies began making their way past the dance floor to the base of the stage.

"What do you think it takes to win the contest?" Marilyn asked.

"The lady who winds this contest will be strong, athletic, and dance slow and erotically," Doc said.

Mako added, "She needs to act like she's making love to that pole. She needs to be able to shimmy up and down that pole like it's a big . . ."

"Mako!" Doc exclaimed interrupting his next few words.

Doc continued, "Like you're making love in a weightless environment."

"Exactly," Mako said in agreement.

"That would take a lot of practice," Marilyn remarked.

The trio watched as each of the twelve contestants gave DJ Ian their song selections and readied themselves for their dances. Ian instructed that they would each be given two minutes of music to perform their routines.

There were varying degrees of skill exhibited in the contest, but only three ladies were real professionals. They definitely understood how to hold your attention.

Mako said that they could "tantalize and make you fantasize."

It was no surprise that the winner was Lila Love. She received a cash prize and an invitation to perform for a whole song later in the evening.

Looking at Marilyn, Doc remarked, "She gives pole dancing lessons early on Wednesday evenings."

"She's got another pupil. I'm going over to talk to her," Marilyn said.

Mako glanced at the weather monitor from time to time noting that the wind was picking up and the barometer was dropping slightly. He mentioned the readings to Doc.

"Hurricane Dani is heading our way. We'll head to the radio room after the fashion show. I think they have six ladies with a couple outfits each," Doc remarked.

Needless to say, the Lust Fashion Show was a winner. The ladies modeled see-through mini dresses, large-net teddies, long lingerie gowns with slits and cutouts, open faced bras with tiny thongs, very small and revealing swimsuits, colorful, full body stockings and many other sexy wear items.

Charlotte announced that Lust would be open until midnight and that there was a special ten percent Hurricane Party discount for tonight only. It didn't take long for a couple dozen customers to make their way to the boutique.

While Doc and Mako reported the updated weather readings to the Hurricane Watch Net, Marilyn took the opportunity to enjoy some fast and slow dances with her friends and neighbors on the big dance floor. DJ Ian provided a good mix of tunes that kept the crowd entertained.

"Charlotte, what's inside that cat shaped piñata that we're breaking at 10:00 pm?" Marilyn inquired.

"It's full of goodies picked especially for this crowd," Charlotte replied.

"You're evading the question," Marilyn said with a grin.

"It's filled with colorful condoms, lubricants, sample non-prescription male enhancement pills, bullet vibrators, and a few eye patches," she reported.

"Eye patches? Why are you giving away eye patches?" Marilyn asked with a puzzled look.

"Oh, honey, that's what we call the small G-strings with the Tampa Bay Buccaneers logo on the front. If a man wins one, he wears it and pretends it's an eye patch – like a pirate," Charlotte explained.

"Arrrrrgh!" Marilyn remarked.

"Be careful. You may have to surrender the booty," Charlotte warned.

Charlotte pointed out that the maintenance crew had placed a small hook on a black rope and attached the piñata to it. At the proper time the cat shaped piñata would be lowered to the center of the dance floor where it could be broken, and its treasures scatted amongst the revelers.

"Who's going to be trying to break the piñata?" Marilyn asked.

"There's not going to be any real trying. We are going to give someone a broomstick and make sure they break it after a couple swings. The fun will be watching everyone scramble for the goodies," Charlotte explained.

"I want to nominate Mako Jenkins. Doc has been mean to him all day. He needs some success and appreciation," Marilyn said.

"You line him up. We'll make sure that he's a hero tonight," Charlotte replied.

When Doc and Mako returned from the radio room their faces were somber. Their demeanor was not indicative of revelers.

"What's wrong, David?" Marilyn asked.

"Based on the reports of ground observers, coupled with atmospheric conditions, it looks like Tampa Bay is in the middle of the area where Hurricane Dani will come ashore," Doc responded.

"It's barely a Category 3 storm and will likely make landfall at a Category 2 storm, but that's still 96 to 110 mph winds," Mako added.

"What will that do?" Charlotte asked.

"It will cause extensive flooding in downtown Tampa, uproot trees, damage buildings, and break windows and doors," Doc replied.

"What do we need to do?" Marilyn asked.

"Steve needs to get security to duct tape large X's across those tall windows in the nightclub, restaurant, and sports bar, and then secure them with that woven polyethylene sheeting," Doc suggested.

"I will grab Gilbert and we'll talk to Steve," Mako said.

"How long do we have before Dani hits land?" Charlotte queried.

"Based on its slow-moving wind speed, I'd guess it'll go ashore around 2:00 to 3:00 am," Doc responded.

"What do you think, Marilyn?" Charlotte asked.

"At 2:00 o'clock in the morning, I'm gonna grab David and we're going to go at it in that double sleeping bag like two drunk monkeys," she replied.

"In a hurricane," Mako added.

"No doubt," Doc said.

DJ Ian stopped the music and asked everyone to listen to the instructions for the Between The Legs Bowling Competition. He promised they wouldn't be complicated.

He instructed those patrons inside Club Fiesta to divide into two groups. Half the customers moved to the left of the large dance floor while the other half moved to the right.

Mako and Doc moved to their right while Marilyn and Charlotte went to the left side of the nightclub. The crowd divided almost perfectly into two equal groups.

"I need each group to choose one bowler to compete in this competition. He or she will be bowling for your group. The competition will be only three rounds with two balls for each round. The best score wins. Each member of the winning group will be given a coupon for one free domestic draft beer.

There will be three ladies who will stand with their legs spread over the bowling lane. The lane edges are marked by red masking tape. The object is to roll the plastic bowling ball between their legs and knock down the plastic bowling pins. If a ball goes outside the lane, that roll will not count," Ian explained.

The group of the left side of Club Fiesta chose Bruno Eberhardt as their designated bowler. He bowled in a league and always had a score of 150 or better.

The group on the right chose Dave McDonald. He was also an excellent bowler and maintained a high game score generally.

As the two bowlers headed to the lane, Doc asked Mako, "What do you think?"

"We're screwed. Bruno has excellent ball control and concentration," Mako opined.

Both Bruno and Dave achieved two strikes each in the two initial attempts. It looked like either one could win the competition.

Just before the third round, the three young women undressed and stood au natural before the bowlers. "This might be a game changer," Doc thought.

Bruno released his ball with a slight amount of hesitation as he glanced at the middle regions of one particularly attractive blonde. His ball went between her legs and struck the head pin only knocking it down and leaving nine pins remaining. His second attempt wasn't much better, but he managed to drop five more pins.

Dave McDonald rolled his plastic bowling ball underneath the same blonde. His ball hit the head pin with great force. When all the pins landed, only two pins remained standing.

He rolled the remaining ball between the legs of the brunette at the right of the lane hoping to take down the split pins. The ball struck one pin sending it into the other pin with both falling over.

"We're drinking a free beer on Steve Riley tonight!" Mako exclaimed.

Dave McDonald was hailed as a hero. Most of the winning group tucked their coupons away for future use. But Mako immediately redeemed his coupon.

Marilyn and Charlotte returned to the right edge of the dance floor to converse with Doc. Marilyn was smiling and so was Charlotte.

"Your man lost. Why are the two of you so happy?" Doc inquired.

"I knew what was going to happen with the girls on the third round. It was guaranteed that the blonde's split was going to earn Bruno a split. He can't resist taking a peek," Charlotte explained.

"So we made side bets of two glasses of wine that Dave would win," Marilyn explained.

"We stopped by to brag on our way to get our glass of wine each," Charlotte said.

As the pair walked toward the bar, Doc said to Mako, "You got two beer coupons, Charlotte and Marilyn got glasses of wine, and I got screwed."

"No you didn't. You'll eat and drink free all night on Steve Riley," Mako reminded.

"God is great. Beer is good. But eating and drinking off Riley is crazy," Doc said rather melodically and pretending to be Billy Currington singing "People Are Crazy."

Doc decided to have his free dinner and enjoy the showing the coconuts and booty shaking until after midnight. Then, it would be back to the Hurricane Net with new observations.

When Doc and Mako returned to the radio room, they discovered that the speed of Hurricane Dani's movement had increased moderately. New calculations put Dani making landfall an hour sooner than expected.

When the net control operator asked for any Tampa stations to report, Doc answered, "W4SRX."

"W4SRX, report," was the response.

"Wind speed now 40 mph sustained with gusts to 55 mph, rain fall at 2.25 inches, and barometric pressure at 28.75. W4SRX," Doc said.

"W4SRX, net control, copy that," the gentleman added.

"What do you think?" Mako asked.

"I'm certainly not a meteorologist but it looks like we're close to a Category 2 storm with Tampa in the vicinity of the eye," Doc said.

"What do we need to do?" Mako said.

"Make sure that Steve knows that the storm will make landfall within the hour and it looks like it's going to be close to a Category 2 here," Doc instructed.

Like clockwork, Hurricane Dani made landfall close to Crystal River, about 55 miles north of downtown Tampa Bay. The barometer was at 28.50 and the sustained winds were about 75 miles per hour and gusting to 90.

Downtown Tampa experienced power outages and some minimal flooding due to the rising tide in Tampa Bay. There were scattered palm fronds but little property damage.

The resort saw wind speeds reach sustained levels at 55 mph and a total rainfall of 5.5 inches. There were some yard chairs and palm fronds strewn around the next morning but nothing but minimal property damage. Caliente never lost power during the storm.

At 2:00 am the party wound down and the revilers started to get a few hours of sleep before breakfast at

7:00 am. The lights were turned down and the music stopped.

Dave McDonald reported to Doc, "There's a very attractive lady in your double sleeping bag waiting for you."

"Sounds like Marilyn missed her chance for us to do the wild thing during the hurricane," Doc remarked.

"It's not Marilyn. It's a blonde," Dave replied.

"Mako, go get that woman handled," Doc instructed.

"I don't know her," Mako responded.

"That's never hindered you getting a woman handled before," Dave McDonald said.

"Go take care of it, Mako," Doc insisted.

"I can't," Mako said.

"Why can't you?" Dave asked.

"I told her she could sleep there," Mako admitted.

"She ain't Goldilocks. Get her ass out of that sleeping bag!" Doc exclaimed.

"You'll have to come with me," Mako insisted.

"Come on, baby bear. Let's relocate Goldilocks," Doc snarled.

When the two men arrived at the double sleeping bag that had been positioned behind the small bar to the right of the dance floor, they found a thirty something, very attractive blonde asleep in the double sleeping bag.

"How do we get her out?" Mako asked.

"You got her in. You figure out how to get her out," Doc said.

"What do you recommend?" Mako asked.

"Here comes Marilyn. Quick, climb in that bag and cover up both your heads till she leaves," Doc instructed.

When Marilyn got closer, Doc saw that she had Mako's wife, Beverly, with her. Months later, Doc remarked that it was the first time he felt that there could easily be a double ass whooping delivered to him and Mako.

"Have you seen, Mako?" Marilyn inquired.

"Why do you ask?" Doc queried.

"I want to get him bedded down for the night," Beverly said.

"I'm thinking that getting him bedded down won't be a problem," Doc responded.

When the blonde in the sleeping bag heard Doc's voice, she threw an arm and a leg around Mako and so, "I've been wanting to have my way with you."

"Who's in that bed?" Marilyn insisted.

"It sure doesn't sound like Goldilocks," Beverly insisted.

Marilyn pulled back the covers and screamed, "Oh Mako! Not Goldilocks!"

"Wait! I can explain. She thought I was Doc and . . . she . . . er, wanted to . . . I mean," Mako stuttered.

Mimicking the Saturday Night Live Church Lady, Dave McDonald said, "Well . . . isn't that special!"

"Did you know about this?" Beverly pointedly asked Doc.

"I can't throw him under the bus. Dave said she was in the sleeping bag. I made Mako come over to get her out. I saw Marilyn coming and I put him under the covers with her to keep from getting a ton of grief from Marilyn. I didn't know that you were heading this way, too," Doc explained.

"If I heard that story from anyone else, I'd think they were covering for Mako, but I believe *you*," Beverly replied.

"I was there and heard the whole thing," Dave added.

"I believe you too, David," Marilyn said as she kissed him on the cheek.

"Hey, why doesn't anyone ever believe me?" Mako asked.

"Because we all know you," Dave replied.

"Mako, I recommend that you get your ass and Goldilocks out of that sleeping bag now," Doc said.

Mako extracted himself from the double sleeping bag and led the lingerie-clad blonde to the piano bar. Dave McDonald excused himself realizing that the discussion wasn't over.

"David, Beverly and I had decided to visit for the next few hours and then have an early breakfast. We were on our way over here to explain our plans," Marilyn said.

"That's not a problem. I'm going to sleep a few hours and then I'll eat with Dave and Mako," Doc opined.

"Are you sharing that bag with Mako?" Beverly asked with a smile.

"Uh, sleeping with Mako is your joy – not mine," Doc replied.

"Tell him what's happening, and encourage him to stay out of trouble," Beverly said.

"I'll have Gilbert keep a watchful eye on him," Doc promised.

After things had settled, Doc took off his shirt, pants and shoes. He climbed into the sleeping bag wearing his boxer shorts and planned on getting a halfway decent night's sleep.

At around 6:45 am the sun started to rise. Doc decided it was time to get dressed and get a free breakfast courtesy of Steve Riley and Caliente Resort.

When Doc turned over to reach his clothes, he looked directly into the face of the girl they had nicknamed Goldilocks.

She said, "Oh, Doc!"

He heard Marilyn say, "Come on Papa Bear. You've got some explaining to do at breakfast."

"I am shocked. I am appalled. This is beyond belief!" Mako remarked.

As Goldilocks left, and Doc dressed and rolled to Café Ole with Marilyn, Mako thought, "I'm a mean man. I am so ashamed of myself . . . NOT!"

17. Behind The Eight Ball

Many years ago Doc took a required college course in business law. He learned a few legal principles about business. One particular legal concept became a part of his psyche. It was mutual assent or a meeting of the minds.

Marilyn's initial encounter with and discussion about the lifestyle was void of a meeting of the minds on the topic. Waver's encounter with Lifestyle Dating Service (LDS) representative's solicitation for membership similarly lacked a meeting of the minds. In fact, the Michaels' considered it to be a dating service for healthy minded individuals.

Fetish Weekend at Caliente had the potential for producing mutual assent for them. In fact, it could bring crystal clarity in some areas.

Doc had developed a healthy interest in Caliente's weekly eight ball pool tournament that was held in the Calypso Cantina on Mondays. He was always a decent pool player but his time at Caliente had sharpened his skills.

On nights where he drew a skilled partner, they would often win the tournament and garner four or five free beer coupons each. Doc would always distribute the coupons to friends or other contestants. He liked pool and he liked winning. He never cared for beer. Waver made sure of that.

On Monday night of Fetish Week at Caliente, the prizes were different. Doc and Marilyn were unaware of the change and no one saw fit to give them instruction.

The Calypso Cantina, Caliente's sports bar, served as a gathering place seven days a week from 11:00 am till at least 9:00 pm nightly. On occasion the fun continued until as late as 11:00 pm.

The bar was encased on three sides with large ceiling to floor glass windows. Even on the coldest days, the bright Florida sunshine kept the bar warm enough to keep the most timid nudist unclothed.

A huge four-sided bar sat in the middle of the large room and had tall bar chairs on all four sides. The patrons at the bar were serviced by a full-time bartender and server.

The rest of the sports bar was filled with tables with chairs for taking meals or just enjoying one's favorite libation. There was a large regulation pool table that was positioned between one side of the four-sided bar and one of the outside glass encased walls.

It was difficult to get a chance at the pool table on cold or rainy days. There were always eight ball aficionados seeking to hone their skills. The best chance for using the pool table was on warm, sunny days when the pools, palm trees, palapas, and lounge chairs beckoned the sun worshipers.

Doc registered for the tournament in the normal way. He and the others drew cards from a deck placed face down and scattered across the pool table. At the end of the draw, those with matching numbers were paired. Once that was done, the remaining players were paired with high card draws versus low card draws.

The Caliente member host would note the teams on a bracket sheet and the play would begin. Two teams of two players were pitted against each other with one team advancing and one team being eliminated by the game's outcome.

Tonight the tournament consisted of one round only for two teams. There was only one game and then the prize was awarded.

Doc did not know any of the other players. He expected that the eight ball tournament was truncated due to the presence of so very many patrons at the resort to celebrate Fetish Week.

A thirty something, blonde haired, muscular gentlemen approached Doc and offered his hand. Doc returned the favor.

"My name is George Thompson. It looks like we're partners," he said.

"I'm David Michaels. I live on the campus," Doc responded.

"You must be very good to play in this tournament," George remarked.

"I'm consistent," Doc said with a chuckle.

"Did you check out those guys wives?" George asked.

"I haven't been introduced to them," Doc said.

"See the hot blonde and the sultry brunette sitting at the end of the bar. That's Molly and Sally. Give them a wave," George said.

Doc and George gave them a wave and the two ladies blew them kisses. Doc thought it strange that their opponents' wives were so friendly to their husbands' competitors. He shrugged it off as the usual Caliente friendliness.

Doc and George won the coin toss and Doc invited George to take the first shot. George sunk two striped balls on the break and continued to drop striped balls fastidiously. When the flurry ended, there was only one striped ball left on the table.

When their opponent took his first shot, the cue ball followed his solid colored ball into the hole. The next shot gave Doc the opportunity to win the game if he could sink the remaining striped ball and then the eight ball.

"If you sink two more balls, we'll be having us some fun tonight," George remarked.

Doc shot a two-rail bank on the thirteen. It hit the center of the corner hole and fell. The cue ball rolled very close to the eight ball and came to rest at a slight angle behind the eight ball about a foot from a side pocket.

"What do you think about that shot?" George asked.

"It is an easy shot but it's also easy for the cue ball to end up down the table in the left corner pocket," Doc opined.

"They have a table full of balls left. It's not likely they will get an eight-ball shot. Maybe I'll get a better shot at the eight ball when it's my turn," George said.

"If I make the shot, we win the game and get our prizes," Doc said.

"If you miss the shot, we'll be sleeping alone tonight," George remarked.

"What do you mean by that?" Doc asked with a puzzled look.

"Our prizes are the hot blonde and the sultry brunette. Their prizes are our wives," George replied.

"I never agreed to that. Marilyn will beat me to death if that happened," Doc said.

"When you signed up for this lifestyle pool tournament, you agreed to those terms. If you want to avoid that beating, you had better sink that eight ball and not lose this game," George warned.

One advantage of being a pool player in a wheelchair is that you are close to the top of the table. You can align your shots and make most close shots with extreme accuracy.

Doc carefully lined up his shot. He kissed the thirteen with the cue ball. The striped ball dropped uneventfully into the side pocket. However, the blue felt tabletop was known for a fast roll and the cue ball continued toward the left corner pocket.

All eyes in the room were on the white ball. Some hoped it would stop and others wanted it to drop into the corner pocket. George was quite unnerved, but Doc was a cool as an early spring morning.

As the white ball moved closer to the left corner pocket, the crowd screamed and cheered. All of a sudden, the cue ball stopped about six inches from the hole.

"We won! We won!" George screamed.

When the noise subsided, Doc looked at George and said, "Find one of those girls a date."

"That won't be a problem. But just out of curiosity, which one would you have chosen? As the game winning partner you'd have had first choice," George asked.

"I have heard that blondes have more fun. But I like sultry brunettes," Doc said with a smile.

Marilyn approached Doc and remarked, "I've never seen that much excitement at this place over a pool game."

"I've never had that much pressure to sink a shot," Doc replied.

"It's just for a free beer, David," Marilyn remarked.

"And my life," Doc muttered as he turned away made his way to their table.

* * *

Doc spent the next few days pondering the predicament into which he had stumbled. He still didn't yet equate his concept of lifestyle with what had happened. However, on certain events, he reasoned that he needed clarification.

The couple's next encounter was on Thursday night for Caliente's weekly Ladies' Night. It was a fun time to dress up in your favorite sexy wear, dance, have interesting conversation with new people, and still make it home by midnight.

When Doc and Marilyn arrived at the Caliente Clubhouse it was packed with patrons. Club Fiesta would open at 8:00 pm and they had reserved a booth with Chadwick. In the interim they found seats in the mostly full piano bar.

Marilyn went to place an order for drinks with Chris, the bartender. Doc opted for his usual Shirley Temple and Marilyn ordered a club soda. She waited at the bar while the drinks were being prepared.

A small framed, mostly white haired, middle age gentlemen approached Doc's table and said, "I'm Mitch Hanson."

Doc replied, "I'm David Michaels. Please, have a seat."

"I want to confess that I'm here on business – plain and simple, Dr. Michaels," Mr. Hanson explained.

"What's the nature of your business?" Doc inquired.

"I'm a bounty hunter," he responded.

"If I understand what you're saying, you hunt down people and receive a fee or bounty," Doc said.

"That is correct. But, I'm not your usual bounty hunter. I'm more like an order taker," Mitch Hanson explained.

"I'm not sure I understand that side of bounty hunting," Doc replied with a confused look on his face.

"It's kind of like running a dating service. People tell me the kind of person they'd like to have for intimate relations, and I do my best to fill the order for an initial fee and then a success bonus," Mr. Hanson explained further.

"I've got the woman that I want she's standing back at the bar talking to that tall, sexy blonde," Doc responded.

"I'm here at Caliente Fetish Week trying to fill a few unusual orders. For example, there is a fetish group composed of both men and women that are referred to as chubby chasers. I'm trying to find a few specific big beautiful women and rotund men for members of that group," Mr. Hanson said.

"What is your compensation for success?" Doc inquired.

"It depends on the level of difficulty and the traits that the client needs. A chubby chaser would normally pay $500 for search and a $500 bonus for a successful match.

However, if someone was wanted a highly specialized person like an athlete, singer, or local celebrity, the fee could easily be as much as $1500 for a search and possibly $1500 for a bonus," Mitch explained.

"I don't mean to be rude but that sounds a lot like pimping," Doc remarked.

"Actually, it's more like brokering since I don't have control of either person. I just try to make the connection and let nature take its course," Mr. Hanson replied with a chuckle.

"How does this concern me?" Doc queried.

"I've got a request for you from the Wheelchair Accessible fetish group. I've been given an initial $1000 retainer," Mr. Hanson replied.

"Let me make sure I understand this correctly. You have been paid $1000 to talk me into having sexual relations with a stranger and hope to make a bonus if it happens," Doc said with incredulity.

"That is partly correctly. I have been given a $1000 retainer. I really don't want to make the connection until late Saturday night," he replied.

"Why on Saturday night and not on Thursday night?" Doc inquired.

"Look at your wife talking to that sexy blonde at the bar," the bounty hunter instructed. About now she's starting to extol the virtues of a relationship with a wheelchair bound man. That's pushing up an increase in the bonus," Mr. Hanson explained.

"Just out of curiosity, what do you expect the price to reach by Saturday night?" Doc asked.

"After tonight we'll be looking at $2,500 and could ultimately reach as much as $5,000," Mitch Hanson opined.

"Well, at least I'm not a *cheap* whore," Doc said with a smile.

"I knew that when I took the job," Mitch said with a laugh.

* * *

"I understand that Dr. Michaels is intelligent, humorous, kind, caring, and committed. But, confidentially, I'd like to ask you a very personal question," the sexy blonde said.

"I'm pretty sure I know what you're going to ask me. It's about the physical relationship," Marilyn replied.

"Share as much information as you can comfortably, please," she implored.

"Were you at the pool tournament on Monday?" Marilyn queried.

"Yes, his technique was superb," the blonde lady opined.

"Honey, if you think that was impressive, his between-the-sheets is a hundredfold better," Marilyn said with a slight boast.

"Oh my!" she replied with a swoon.

"For real," Marilyn replied.

* * *

Marilyn returned to the table with the two drinks. Mitch Hanson ended his conversation with Doc as he saw her leaving the bar.

"Who was that fellow?" Marilyn asked.

"He's a bounty hunter," Doc responded.

"Is he looking for someone at Caliente?" Marilyn inquired.

"Actually, he's looking for several people," Doc said.

"I was afraid this Fetish Weekend would draw a few miscreants," Marilyn remarked.

"I'd bet that Mr. Mitch Hanson usually finds the man or woman that's the object of his search," Doc opined.

* * *

Just after 8:00 pm Chadwick alerted the couple that booth was available. Marilyn made her way to the booth on the left side of the large dance floor. Doc made his way through the crowd carefully piloting his wheelchair.

As he neared the booth, he was stopped by the sexy blonde who had been conversing with Marilyn in the piano bar. Doc would later say that she had the look of a wanton seductress.

"My name is Janine. I'm the president of the group Wheelchair Accessible," the sexy blonde explained.

"I am Dr. David Michaels. How can I help you?" Doc inquired politely.

"There are a few of us that would like to have a dance or two and get to know you better. We're very interested in . . . wheelchair accessibility," she explained.

"I don't mind a dance or two, but you really need to discuss that with my wife. She's known to be the jealous type," Doc suggested.

"We'll give you a chance to get settled and then I'll speak with her," Janine promised.

When Doc reached the booth, Marilyn inquired, "What did Janine want?"

"She and a friend wanted a dance with me," Doc responded.

"What did you tell her?" Marilyn asked.

"I told her to take that up with you because you are the jealous type," Doc said.

"David, you are a grown-ass man! If you didn't want to dance with her you should have handled it yourself and not dumped it off on me," Marilyn rebuked.

Before Doc could reply, Mako showed up at the booth, scooted Marilyn to the inside, and took a seat. He was visibly excited about something.

"I heard about your tournament victory on Monday night! Your last shot and that win is now legendary," Mako exclaimed.

"That shot caused a lot of excitement," Marilyn added.

"How was the prize? Was it better than two beer coupons?" Mako teased.

"Like always, I gave the prize away," Doc replied.

"Oh, Doc! You didn't give the prize away! I could just cry!" Mako replied with a definite whine in his voice.

"Don't worry dear. I'll make sure he gives you the prize next time," Marilyn promised.

"Will you, Doc? Would you do that for your best buddy?" Mako pleaded.

"I will," Doc said.

Mako jumped out of his seat, ran toward Doc and gave him a bear hug before leaving the booth. Doc looked around to see if many people in Club Fiesta noticed the incident.

"Can you believe he got that excited over a pool tournament prize?" Marilyn asked.

"I got really excited about it myself," Doc said with raised eyebrows.

18. Caliente Pirate Festival (Part I)

One of the best annual events at Caliente Resort is its Pirate Festival held on the third weekend in October. Folklore says that in the 1700s one or more pirate ships operated in the Gulf waters west of Tampa Bay.

The annual festivities at the three-day event include several local bands, a pirate ball in Club Fiesta, a pirate-decorated golf cart parade, Best Wench contest based on the costume and the booty, an amateur video contest, and a dozen or more vendors selling costumes, jewelry, crafts, and other merchandise.

Doc and Marilyn decided to forego Thursday's Ladies Night at the club to carefully prepare for the three-day pirate festival. Marilyn focused on a costume in hopes of winning the Best Wench contest. Doc, on the other hand, wanted to help Dave McDonald decorate and win the Golf Cart Show & Parade.

Mako convinced Marilyn to permit him to enter a couple of her one-minute Miss Tittie videos in the amateur video contest. The rules were simple:

> 1. Any number of videos, to a maximum of five, could be entered but their aggregate time could not exceed five minutes.

2.   The videos could contain tasteful nudity,
be sexy, and be provocative, but they could
not be obscene.

3.   The videos will be shown on Saturday
afternoon before the Best Wench contest.

Marilyn's 'Miss Tittie' videos were one-minute bare
breast vignettes on a particular theme. There was a total
of 36 videos in the Miss Tittie series and Mako was
picking out the five that he felt had the best chance of
impressing the judges.

The video that Mako thought was the best was
entitled, "Watermelon." In the video Marilyn was
standing at a kitchen counter with a large knife in hand
near a large round watermelon.

As the scene opened, Marilyn said, "This is Miss
Tittie and I am cutting watermelon."

Marilyn begins to actually cut the watermelon and
continues, "I like cutting watermelon because it makes
my titties go bob, bob, bob!"

Her full, natural breasts somewhat swayed with the
cutting process and she ended the video with a huge
smile signifying a pleasant and successful watermelon
cutting.

The four other one-minute videos that Mako selected
for contest entry were:

1. Panties in the Freezer, similar to a Marilyn
Monroe scene in the film, "The Seven Year Itch,"

2. Tittie Wash, a video that is self-explanatory,

3. The Top is Down, a video about being topless in a convertible, and,
4. Titillation, a silent video, with background music, suggesting its own subject matter.

Doc was aware of Mako's efforts but didn't believe that the videos would make it to one of the top three places in the contest.

* * *

Doc suggested that Dave McDonald decorate his golf cart as though it belonged to the Tampa Bay Buccaneers. He had arranged for four of his female friends to wear Tampa Bay Buccaneer cheerleader costumes.

Unknown to Dave, Doc had arranged for the girls to lift their short skirts and moon the crowd at certain intervals along the parade route. He also planned for the cheerleaders to moon the judges near the finish line of the golf cart parade.

After almost a year at the luxury, clothing optional resort, Doc knew that success in any endeavor at Caliente required that some portion of the option had to be exercised.

The Pirate Festival began at high noon on Friday. When the patrons entered the clubhouse it was decorated like a pirate ship. Rum was the preferred drink of the day. The servers, clad in pirate attire, greeted the customers as they entered the building.

Lust Boutique offered a lot of pirate wear, jewelry, temporary body decals and henna tattoos. They advertised "Wench Wear" to the patrons.

Outside the building a large swath of vendors surrounded the pool area. They offered all types of goods and services. The crowd favorites seem to be tiny skull & cross bones pirate thongs, pirate themed body painting, and pirate themed body jewelry.

The bands changed every two hours from noon until 6:00 pm. The genres were mostly 70s and 80s oldies, classic rock, and pop.

Doc entered the handicap gate near the outdoor showers. One of Marilyn's friends, Meredith Webster, wearing only a pirate wench body painting, straddled Doc in his wheelchair. Before Doc could say anything, Meredith exclaimed, "I'm surrendering the booty, baby!"

"That may be the rum talking, Meredith," Doc remarked.

"I've drunk you pretty already, Doc," she explained.

It wasn't long before her husband showed up to greet Doc and Marilyn. It appeared that his wife was quite happy wiggling around in Doc's lap.

"I've got something that belongs to you," Doc said.

As he helped his wife out of Doc's lap, her husband remarked, "It's the Bacardi 151."

"Doc thought it was his good looks and pleasing personality," Marilyn added.

"I'm sure that didn't hurt," he said with a chuckle.

"I'll wait here for Dave and Mako while you shop," Doc explained.

"Why do you think I'm going shopping?" Marilyn asked.

"Because you brought your clutch purse and the resort is cashless. You intend to shop the vendors' goods and services," Doc remarked.

"You are sooo cerebral, David," Marilyn said as she walked toward the vendor line.

"Damn! According to her, I'm personable, good looking, and cerebral. No wonder I have wenches climbing on me," Doc said with slight sarcasm.

* * *

Doc took a path in the opposite direction Marilyn chose. He thought he might find something special for her in all the treasures.

Doc noticed a small, thin, well-built Latin lady approaching him. He recognized her as one of the seasonal regulars at Caliente. It was Maritza Martin. She was waving frantically at Doc. He stopped his chair and waited for her.

"Doc, I really need a favor," Maritza said.

"How can I help you sweet lady?" Doc asked.

"There is a $10 entry fee for the oil wrestling competition. They won't take cash and I'm not a member. I'm just a visitor. I need you to sponsor me," she explained.

"What is your category?" Doc asked.

233

"I'm in the lightest category: 48 kilograms or 105 pounds," Maritza replied.

"Let's go get you enrolled," Doc said.

Once the registration was completed, Maritza gave Doc a big hug and a long, wet kiss. It was noticed by many of those in the Tiki Bar and winter pool area.

Maritza waved and remarked in a Terminator voice, "I'll be back."

As Doc nodded, Mako arrived on the scene. Doc knew that it wouldn't be long before he was subjected to a Mako cross examination.

"What did you do to get a face full of her?" Mako inquired.

"I paid $10 to sponsor her in the lightweight division of the oil wrestling competition," Doc replied.

"I'm sticking around to see if she wins the $150 prize," Mako said.

"Are you a wrestling fan?" Doc queried.

"Not necessarily. I just want to see what she gives you for a $150 win," Mako said.

"Mako, you are immutable," Doc responded.

"Is that good or bad?" Mako queried.

"It means you never change," Doc said.

"That's good! I am very consistent," Mako beamed.

Marilyn walked up to the two men and asked, "So what earned you all that public affection from Maritza?"

"He sponsored her in the oil wrestling competition. He paid her entry fee," Mako explained.

"It's another CNN reporter on site giving slanted coverage," Doc remarked.

"Are you betting on a little side action, David?" Marilyn asked with a smirk.

"I'm waiting to see what he gets when she wins the $150 prize," Mako said excitedly.

"I'm interested in that, too," Marilyn replied.

Changing the subject, Doc asked, "Speaking of wenches, are you registered for the Best Wench contest?"

"As a matter of fact, I am," Marilyn replied.

"Do you think I can win?" Marilyn asked.

"What do you think, Mako?" Doc asked hoping that Mako would give a bad answer.

"She needs to drop those panties," Mako opined.

"Why? As Waver says, the judges would see Christmas," Marilyn remarked.

"That's the point, Marilyn. It's what the French call lagniappe or a little extra," Doc replied.

"I'll think about it," Marilyn said.

"Think about that $300 first place prize," Mako said as Marilyn continued making her trek to the remaining vendors.

"Doc, if both of those women win, I can be your back up guy," Mako remarked.

"You've got all you can handle. I've heard that some days you've got more than you can handle," Doc said tongue-in-cheek.

"Who told you that? Did Beverly say something to you? Don't you know that's just rank gossip and hearsay?" Mako asked in rapid succession.

"As an acting CNN guy, you certainly realize that I can't reveal my sources," Doc said as he turned toward the Tiki Bar. Mako stood there shaking his head and fuming.

* * *

Doc rolled his wheelchair underneath the low side of the counter of the Tiki Bar. He placed an order for his usual Shirley Temple. He listened to the live band playing their version of Rod Stewart's, "Do Ya Think I'm Sexy?"

A very beautiful and sexy blonde stepped beside Doc and asked, "Do ya?"

"I beg your pardon?" Doc replied.

"Do you think I'm sexy?" the lady replied.

"If you look up sexy in the dictionary, your picture is there," Doc replied.

"That's an old one," she said with a smile.

"I could have asked if you've ever made love to a man in a wheelchair?" Doc said hoping to shock her.

"No, but I'm game," she replied.

"I'm obviously under matched for verbal sparring with you. I'm David Michaels," Doc said.

"Actually, you are Dr. David Michaels, an oral surgeon. I'm Samantha Simpson," the beautiful blonde said.

"I wasn't aware that we had met," Doc said.

"You are the guy that avoided the drive by on the night of Hurricane Dani," Samantha offered.

"What drive by? I'm not sure what you mean?" Doc queried.

"Remember the girl you called Goldilocks? She climbed into your sleeping bag looking to do the wild thing with someone she didn't personally know. A lot of folks around here call that a drive by," Samantha explained.

"Was it unusual that she wanted a drive by or that I didn't want a drive by?" Doc asked.

"Buy me a Shirley Temple and I'll spill my guts," Samantha said with a smile.

Dave McDonald had been looking for Doc for about an hour. He finally located him in the Tiki Bar engaged in meaningful conversation with Samantha.

"Doc, I need to speak with you about the golf cart," Dave said.

"Ask me anything. I want to get back to Samantha's tell all," Doc said with a silly smile.

"I mean I need to show you something before the golf cart parade," Dave insisted.

"Duty calls, sweet lady. Maybe we can catch each other later this weekend," Doc said.

"I'm counting on it," Samantha said while giving Doc a cute little goodbye wave.

After Doc had rolled past most of the end of the large pool, Dave put his hand on Doc's shoulder to get him to stop. When Doc looked at Dave, he had an unusual expression on his face.

"Doc, how well do you know Samantha?" Dave inquired.

"I was getting to know her quite well until you showed up with a golf cart issue," Doc replied.

"Doc, I don't think that she's what you think," Dave opined.

"She's sexy, beautiful, intelligent, and has a great personality. What else is there to worry about?" Doc asked.

"She's got a penis," Dave said bluntly.

"I'm waiting for the rest of the story on the point you're trying to make," Doc replied.

"She's a transsexual. Now that's her business, but you need to know that before you go all schoolboy on her," Dave remarked.

"I don't care what type of equipment she has or doesn't have. I don't intend on testing it now or ever. It's hard to find good, decent, and, caring people these days regardless of their gender or gender preference," Doc said.

"Doc, I didn't . . .," Dave said before being interrupted.

"I saw her little secret bulging in that bikini. I enjoyed her company. I appreciate your concern. I'm not offended," Doc said.

Marilyn appeared beside Doc as he finished his conversation with Dave McDonald. She was in a happy and excited mood.

"What have you been up to?" Marilyn asked.

"Having a Shirley Temple with a very beautiful transsexual," Doc admitted.

"You must mean Samantha. She's a wonderful person," Marilyn said.

"Aren't you afraid I'll run off with her?" Doc asked rather sarcastically.

"She's a blonde. You like sultry brunettes like me," she replied.

19. Caliente Pirate Festival (Part II)

Mako appeared at the group and said, "Hey! The oil wrestling competition is about to begin. Maritza's up first."

The group returned to the winter pool area. There was a large inflatable pool about 24 inches deep, six foot wide, and eight feet long. It was filled with vegetable oil.

The object of the match was to strip your opponent and pin her for at least a three count. Usually the tiny bikini tops didn't last long. The loss of the bikini bottom wasn't far behind.

The time set for each match was five minutes. If a contestant had been stripped and another had some clothing intact, the naked wrestler was the loser. If both contestants were naked but neither had been pinned for a three count, the winner would be chosen by the three judges.

There was a referee that managed the wrestling to keep the competition clean. He also served as an interpreter of the specialized Caliente oil wrestling rules.

Maritza steeped into the inflated and oil filled ring waiting on her opponent. One other lady in the 98 kg/105 pound had registered to compete.

After a minute or two, one of the judges called the opposing contestant to the match. A minute later he made a second call.

The referee lifted Maritza's arm to signify that she was the winner by default. She was so excited that she jerked off her small bikini top and rolled around in the oil. The crowd cheered and clapped for her success and subsequent victory celebration.

Maritza saw Doc and rushed toward him. She jumped into his lap and gave him a bear hug and a long, rather passionate, kiss.

Mako said, "I knew it! I *knew* it! She's gonna rub all over him!"

"At least that oil will prevent him from overheating," Marilyn remarked.

After the momentary excitement had abated, Maritza left the group and made her way to the judges' area to claim her $150 prize. She was officially the Caliente Oil Wrestling champion in her weight class.

"It's time to go home," Doc said.

"Nooooo! It about time for the Pirate Video Contest," Mako exclaimed.

"Your degreasing will have to wait," Dave McDonald said.

The sun was sinking behind the horizon and it was just getting dark enough to get a good look at the video presentations. A large crowd had gathered around the large waterfall pool.

An inflatable screen with a large white painted surface had been set at the waterfall end of the pool. It was a great spot for the most festival participants to view the videos.

One of the judges motioned for Mako to come to the judges' area. Everyone wondered what was happening.

"He's been disqualified," Doc opined.

"Why would you say that?" Marilyn asked with a shocked look.

"Those Miss Tittie videos are just too hot for this crowd," he replied.

"I don't think anything is too hot for this rowdy bunch," Dave McDonald opined.

"What did they want?" Doc asked.

"I can't say," Mako responded.

"What do you mean by that?" Doc asked rather impatiently.

"I can't reveal my sources and I've promised to keep the information confidential," Mako said smugly.

On the large screen appeared a panel that said Caliente Pirate Video Contest. It was accompanied by some loud, epic sounding music.

Like clockwork the contest opened with the Miss Tittie series: Watermelon, Freezer Panties, Tittie Wash, Top Down, and Titillation.

The crowd clapped, cheered, and whistled as the five minutes of Miss Tittie videos came to an end. Marilyn was a little self-conscious and a little embarrassed at the attention from several hundred Pirate Festival attendees.

One of the judges had obtained a microphone and raised his hand to silence the crowd. It seemed unusual that the judges would stop the show in the midst of the competition.

He began, "The judges reviewed the five contestants' submission to the contest. Some had content that we felt exceeded the boundaries set by the contest rules. One was voluntarily withdrawn because it was submitted without the permission of the model.

Therefore, the Miss Tittie montage is declared the winner!"

The crowd clapped, cheered, and screamed in favor of the announcement. In fact, there were some calls to show it again.

Mako grabbed Marilyn, gave her a tight bear hug, and gave her a long, excited kiss. Doc knew he'd get to talk about this for at least a couple of weeks.

The judge raised his hand to quiet the crowd. Everyone was curious as to what the next announcement would say.

"When the contestants submitted their selections for this contest, we asked them to submit an additional short video of no more than two minutes in duration. The additional video would be shown in behalf of the contestant placing first in the contest," he explained.

No one knew which of the other almost forty video clips that Mako had submitted in case of a win. They held their breath waiting for the title.

"Mako Jenkins has submitted an additional Miss Tittie video, entitled, Mouse Tattoo."

"Oh, Mako! You didn't! This is naughty!" Marilyn whined.

"I didn't realize she had a tattoo," Dave McDonald remarked.

"You're about to find out why," Doc replied.

The Mouse Tattoo video began with a nude from the waist up Marilyn remarking, "Hey! Did you know I have a little tattoo? It's right down here."

The camera slowly moved to her smooth middle regions.

Marilyn then said, "It's a little mouse."

After it lingers for a moment or two and there is no mouse tattoo, Marilyn said with shocked expression, "Oh no! My pussy ate it!"

The camera pans back to a shot of her from the waist up. Her smile has turned into a look of utter surprise.

She shrugged and said, "Oh well!"

The crowd noise was deafening. Marilyn hid her face. Mako jumped with joy. Dave McDonald broke into uncontrollable laughter.

From that day forward, Marilyn became totally known as Miss Tittie. She said, several months later, that on judgment day she'd be called up by the name Miss Tittie rather than Marilyn Michaels.

Marilyn looked directly at Doc and said, "You're right. It's time to go home."

Doc and Marilyn headed for the gate as the sun sunk behind the palm trees. Mako made his way to the judges' area to pick up his winnings. The band on the stage crooned and played Montgomery Gentry's version of Titty's Beer.

* * *

After a long first day of Caliente's Pirate Festival, Doc and Marilyn spent a quiet evening at 69 Sandhill Crane Drive. Mako could contain his enthusiasm so about 8:00 pm he had to come by and offer to share his $300 winnings with Marilyn.

"Now Marilyn I'll gladly split this money with you," Mako offered.

"No way," Doc replied.

"I agree but what makes you say that, David?" Marilyn queried.

"You should be paying Mako. His hard work has turned you into a Caliente superstar. Steve Riley may offer to pay you to just stand around and show those beautiful breasts," Doc replied.

"I better leave. He's working it up," Mako remarked.

"He's doing a pretty good job, too," Marilyn responded.

* * *

At noon on Saturday, Dave McDonald rang the doorbell. Marilyn answered the door wearing a pair of distressed denim shorts that offered a solid view of her buns.

She had donned a matching short denim vest that was barely able to be fastened by the two large metal buttons on the front. The pedicure on her bare feet completed the look.

"It's about an hour before the Best Wench contest. Looks like you're ready," Dave said.

"I've got to go get ready," Marilyn replied.

"Get ready? What's this?" Dave inquired.

"This is Doc's version of Surrender The Booty," Marilyn replied.

"Did you surrender the booty?"

"Aaaarrrgh!" Marilyn growled.

As she walked toward the master bedroom, Dave thought, "That sounded like a yes."

"Doc, are you ready?" Dave said loudly.

Doc rolled out of the master bedroom not wearing anything but a smile. He gave Dave McDonald his trademark one eye closed, head tilted downward Doc look.

"I was till you showed up," Doc said.

"What do you mean?" Dave asked.

Mako, who had just stepped through the front door, said, "You cock blocked him. It was a coitus cut-offus pure and simple."

"Thank you for that reasoned diagnosis, Dr. Lust," Doc replied.

"I'm sorry but the golf car parade starts before the Best Wench contest. We have to go now," Dave explained.

"I'm not riding in the cart," Doc replied.

"Steve wants you to be leading the parade in your wheelchair," Dave said with a smile.

"Oh, those women will go wild over that Teddy Bear look," Mako teased.

"Let's go. I'm sitting in this wheelchair. They can't see my junk anyway," Doc said.

Mako grabbed his chest and exclaimed, "It's the big one. Doc is exercising the option. He's going out buck naked. This is exciting news!"

"Wait! Wait!" Marilyn said as she continued, "I can't miss this historic moment."

"That's why Steve wants you to lead the parade," Dave said with a laugh.

When he arrived at the parade route, he discovered that he was going to be pushed along by last year's Best Wench winner, Lila Love.

"If I'd known you were going au natural, I wouldn't have worn this pirate thong," Lila said to Doc.

"Throw caution to the wind and rip it off," Doc insisted.

Following Doc's instruction, Lila ripped off the pirate thong and tossed it into the crowd. It landed on the head of a spectator who pulled it across his one eye and wore it as a dutiful buccaneer.

The crowd loved the spontaneity. Even Doc clapped at the turn of events.

"That's why Steve Riley calls Doc a fixture. There's always fun when he's around," Mako remarked.

"He's definitely a hand full," Marilyn said.

The golf cart parade made its way from one side of the clubhouse, through spectator lined campus, and returned to the other said of the clubhouse. The four faux cheerleaders did their share of flashing and performed their grand finale just as Dave McDonald's Bucs inspired cart made it across the finish line.

When the results were announced, there was no surprise. Dave McDonald won the contest hands down.

"What did you get? Was it a big fat check?" Mako asked.

"He gets to park his cart in the special reserved parking space at the front of the clubhouse near the marble lions," Doc explained.

"What good is that?" Mako asked.

"When I leave the clubhouse, I don't have to walk my tired ass down the hill to my golf cart for a whole year," Dave explained.

The group went through the clubhouse and outside to the large complex that supported four of the five swimming pools, hundreds of lounge chairs, and dozens of palapas. Saturday's crowd was larger than yesterday.

The Best Wench judge interrupted the local band, Stone Feather and it's lead singer, Chuckster, to call the beauty contestants to the outdoor stage. It was about 15 minutes before the contest was slated to start.

Doc, Mako, and Dave had already positioned themselves between the waterfall end of the large pool and the outdoor stage. It was the best vantage point for viewing the hot wenches.

When he saw Marilyn approaching, Dave said, "They're calling for you."

"That's why I came to find Doc and give him these," Marilyn replied as she handed Doc her tiny black pirate thong. She had taken it from underneath her pirate wench costume. Her almost totally visible breasts were sitting atop an open-faced push up bra hidden behind the vest.

"I guess it's getting close to Christmas," Mako remarked.

"You've spent too much time around Waver," Marilyn replied.

"Looks like you might get over exposed with Mako's topless video contest and that pirate costume that yells, "I'll 'Surrender The Booty,'" Doc opined.

Marilyn walked to the judge and had a brief conversation. She returned to the group wearing a large smile.

"Did you get your position number?" Dave asked.

"I dropped out of the contest," Marilyn replied.

"Oh, No! Not the best wench!" Mako whined mimicking Marilyn's trademark shock response.

"David is right. We get too much exposure around here. Winning the Pirate Video Contest and being proclaimed Miss Tittie is enough notoriety for a while.

"But Marilyn, you'll miss a chance at the honor, the glory, and the prize money." Mako continued to whine.

"It's once a year. They'll forget by next year's festival," Marilyn replied.

Doc and Marilyn spent a couple hours at the Pirate Ball and enjoyed the time with their friends and neighbors. Much to Marilyn's chagrin, Mako had put her five videos plus the bonus mouse tattoo video on small thumb drives and was selling them for $9.95 plus an 8 x 10 color photo of a very scantily clad Marilyn from one of Caliente Resort's social media posts.

"If he's anything, he's enterprising," Doc remarked about Mako.

"That's one of the many things I like about him," Marilyn said.

"He's my best friend," Doc replied.

CPSIA information can be obtained
at www.ICGtesting.com
Printed in the USA
LVHW021938210619
622026LV00006B/43/P